ADVANCE PRAISE FC  E

"This compact but mighty collection explores both the heights and depths of the unsavory business of being human. With exquisite, emotionally rich prose, every story surprises and unsettles. Tenderness coexists with terror, beauty alongside betrayal. Characters are at turns earnest and terrible as they grapple with longing, lust, grief, regret, and disappointment. The heart of this brilliant collection is chaos––the way the universe is chaotic, unpredictable, and simply dazzling."

DEESHA PHILYAW
author of *The Secret Lives of Church Ladies*
and finalist for the National Book Award

"Reading this very brilliant debut feels like holding a live wire, receiving a kind of shock our current literature seldom gives. It's a shock we need. Kelly Sather's characters, seeking escape from unbearable lives, are canny, naïve, cruel, bewildered, sometimes a little despicable, always entirely human—and utterly indifferent to our sympathy. *Small in Real Life* has a rare wisdom, born of freedom from illusions most of the rest of us can't bear to let go of. This is among the most impressive new books of fiction I have read in years."

GARTH GREENWELL
author of *Cleanness*

"*Small in Real Life* is a heart-piercing and haunting debut. Kelly Sather is a writer possessed of rare courage—the courage to render our darkest tendencies *and* the last flicker of light we are terrified to lose. Each of these gorgeous, unflinching stories is the shard of a broken mirror, refracting pieces of our impossible lives, showing us what we've done and what we look like right now."

BRET ANTHONY JOHNSTON
author of *Remember Me Like This*

"In Kelly Sather's phenomenal short story collection, she compresses the daily commotion of life into riveting moments of reckoning, whether earned or forced. Desire can obscure or illuminate, and in these compelling stories, Sather's characters deal with the complications of wanting and existing in the world. Sentence by sentence, *Small in Real Life* is one of the best debuts I've ever read."

MICHELE FILGATE
editor of *What My Mother and I Don't Talk About*

"Kelly Sather is a clear-eyed observer. These stories remind the readers of the thrills and dangers of living, and that we are never far from the undercurrent of human emotions, both mysterious and meaningful."

YIYUN LI
author of *The Book of Goose*

SMALL IN REAL LIFE

SMALL REAL

KELLY SATHER

IN
LIFE

STORIES

University of Pittsburgh Press

Published by the University of Pittsburgh Press, Pittsburgh, Pa., 15260

This paperback edition, Copyright © 2024, Kelly Sather

Copyright © 2023, Kelly Sather

All rights reserved

Manufactured in the United States of America

Printed on acid-free paper

10 9 8 7 6 5 4 3 2 1

Cataloging-in-Publication data is available from the Library of Congress

ISBN 13: 978-0-8229-6734-7

ISBN 10: 0-8229-6734-0

Cover art: Seth Armstrong, *The Delivery*, 2021. Oil on wood panel, 72 × 48 inches.

Cover design: Joel W. Coggins

For Amelia, Wyatt, and Oliver

people here
have become
the people
they're pretending to be

7/27/81
Los Angeles, Ca.
Sam Shepard

CONTENTS

❋   ❋   ❋

SMALL IN REAL LIFE

THE SPANIARD

*   *   *

Two days before Jenny's sixteenth birthday she got sick at school.
They couldn't reach her mother, so they gave her bus fare and sent her
home on the RTD. She had chills and her head hurt, but she wasn't
throwing up. We don't want those germs around here, the school secretary had said. It wasn't unusual to send a sick kid out the school gates with
a dollar fifty in her pocket. On the bus, Jenny leaned her head against the
tinted brown glass. Los Angeles, April 1984, palm trees and cement
drifted past her window. She thought about her bed, her comforter with
pink roses. She felt its soft, quilted cotton press against her cheek.

When Jenny got home, her mother's Volvo was parked in the driveway.
No one answered the doorbell. She walked around the house, through the
gate to the backyard. She slid the pot of her mother's white petunias and
picked up the key hidden underneath, though when she tried the back
door, she found it unlocked. She walked through the laundry room, down
a narrow hall toward the kitchen, where she would get a glass of water on
the way to her bedroom. Suddenly, in the middle of the silent house, she

heard a girlish twitter, unfamiliar, yet she knew it was her mother's voice. Her mother must be on the phone.

But in the kitchen, her mother faced the miniature espresso machine, watching coffee drip into a tiny cup. She wore a waistless baby doll dress that showed off her tennis legs. Pink satin with white-laced edges. A dark-haired man with glowing olive skin sat at the kitchen table, smoking a cigarette, plate of ashes by his right hand. He nodded at Jenny like she was a fellow patron at the coffee shop looking for a table, and cleared his throat. A foreigner in a foreign land, Jenny thought, and then, as two streams of gray wisp blew out the man's polished nose, *Smoking kills.*

Her mother nearly dropped the little cup on her way to serve it.

"What are you doing here?" she said.

"I'm sick."

"Oh." Her mother looked her over. Jenny wondered if she looked sick. She slumped her shoulders forward.

"This is my friend Federico," her mother said.

Jenny turned to the olive-skinned man. "Hello, Federico."

He bowed his shiny black head toward her.

"It is a pleasure to meet you. I did not know that Celia's daughter has the same fire eyes." His accent leaned on the *Ce* in *Celia* so it sounded like "Seeeeeeeee-ya." Jenny's eyes were brown like her father's, Celia's hazel. Federico brought the tiny cup to his lips and drank his espresso in one swig. "And now," he said, as if he were a magician about to conjure a rabbit from the pocket of his sleek trousers, "I must leave you beautiful ladies." His teeth were pure white.

Federico paused in the doorway and raised his hand in a flat palm wave, then the front door thudded shut. Celia stood flushed and preening in the middle of the yellow-tiled kitchen. Jenny pulled a glass from the cupboard and held its wide mouth under the tap.

"I want a car for my birthday, or I'm telling Dad."

✳   ✳   ✳

"Federico may not be Spanish," Sam said. Jenny's brother slid his finger down the list of Member States in his *Model UN Handbook*. Jenny and Sam were eighteen months apart, Irish twins, their mother called them, as if they were a gang sent to torment her. Sam was fourteen, younger and smarter. In Model UN, Sam represented Belize, a new Member State, with a Caribbean, British, and Latin American history. And that's not even considering the undersized but oil-rich country's Mayan ancestry, he would add. Belize had a small population, with sugarcane, bananas, barrier reefs, and oil deposits. Sam worked hard to establish liaisons in support of their tourism and export industries. It turned out that Belize was a Commonwealth nation, and Sam was the only ninth grader in the United States, Jenny assumed, with a poster of Queen Elizabeth II on the back of his bedroom door.

Sam frowned at the next page of Member States. "He could be Argentinian, or Brazilian. At the fall conference, I met a kid at the water fountain who called himself Federico, and he was the Italian ambassador."

Sam's Belizean name was Sam.

"Does it really matter which one?" Jenny wanted to talk about the car, her car.

"They're Latin, southern cultures. The men are passionate lovers. If he were from England, say, or Canada . . ." Sam leaned back in his chair and pushed a foot off his desk to send the chair spinning.

"What?"

"He might confuse lust with love and marry her. We'd have a broken home." Sam said *passionate lovers* and *lust* and *broken home* without a snicker. He assimilated details like a calculator figured numbers. Her parents deferred to him when they purchased appliances. Sam was partial to Whirlpool and KitchenAid.

"He's Latin," Jenny said. She stretched out on Sam's bed. She was a full-bodied girl, marooned in this sunny land of California waifs, nymphs like her mother. Mr. T the Cat slept on Sam's pillow. She pulled Mr. T onto her stomach, which had started to ache, though the chills had stopped, and Mr. T curled into a ball.

Sam spun and spun in the chair, his eyes on the ceiling.

"Federico wears cologne," Jenny said. "He stinks like that skunk in the cartoon who falls in love with the white cat." Though she had only smelled smoke coming off Federico, and the slight soapy scent of her father after he showered.

"Pepé Le Pew is French," Sam said. "If you tell Dad, he'll move out." His hazel eyes, their mother's eyes, lit up. "I bet I could get a sailboat," he said. The fathers always moved out to condos in the Marina.

"So Mom won't get me the car, Dad's leaving, and you're getting a boat?"

"I see," Sam said, studying her. "You're going with Idle Threat." He enunciated so she could feel the capitalization.

"Far from idle," Jenny said.

She'd wanted a car every second of every day since the wearisome horrors of high school. Jenny had fallen between the cliques. She was lazy for the smart kids, shy for the theater freaks, klutzy for sports, and the druggies resented her sarcasm. The car would be her own land, her territory of oneness. She was a loser walking the sidewalks alone. On the road in a car, *wearing sunglasses*, she was someone else. Her sixteenth birthday: her car in the driveway wrapped in a bow like on TV. She imagined driving the coast highway in her red VW Scirocco, thick, salty air whipping her face. Her freedom and her mother's penance bound together at sixty miles per hour.

Sam watched the queen staring at them from the back of his bedroom door. He nodded slowly to Elizabeth II. Jenny liked to assume Sam was with her, a twin on her side as her mother claimed, and yet he ran a sovereign nation. He had negotiated favorable trade agreements for a third world country with the prime minister of Great Britain.

"What if she doesn't believe you?" he said.

"She believes me," Jenny said. She patted Mr. T harder on the head, dragging his cat eyes wide open with the force of her palm.

Sam put the tips of his fingers together and gazed into their emptiness.

"What if she doesn't care?" he said.

Jenny thought of her mother in the pink silk dress, her eyes specked with yellow light, her wavy brown hair rolling down the middle of her back. Her mother had the legs and the temperament, the hair and the golden eyes (wasted on Sam), for husbands and Federicos, Canadians and Englishmen.

"She better care," Jenny said.

*   *   *

Her father was home for dinner, sitting at the table where Federico had stubbed out his Camel or Lucky Strike or, more likely, Marlboro Man cigarette. Her mother was doling out soggy lumps of chicken chow mein

7

onto the plate in front of him when the phone rang. Jenny leaned back in her chair and picked up the receiver hanging on the wall. She watched her mother, but her mother was looking down at the chow mein, slopping the brown mess onto Sam's plate.

"Hello?" Jenny said. *Federico?*

The caller waited a few seconds, and then she heard the click of the receiver.

"They hung up."

Her mother sat down beside her father. She pinned squishy noodles, sprouts, and water chestnuts with her fork, while her dad eyed Jenny as if he were in on her joke, as if she had one. Her father had the straightforward gaze, capable gait, and quick, hungry smile of a fighter pilot. He'd joined the Air Force to avoid the draft. Sam annoyed her when he pointed out that their father never flew anything, not even a bug-eyed Bell helicopter.

"A hanger-upper, eh?" her father said, and swept a pile of water chestnuts into his mouth.

"If it was for me, they would've said something." Jenny sipped her chicken broth and nibbled at the toast her mother had prepared for her tender stomach.

"Not if he didn't have the nerve," he said. He sat back and raised his thick eyebrows at Jenny. He wasn't tan like Federico, but he understood his appeal; in that way, they were comparable. He had strong shoulders. Her father thought boys called girls, even girls who looked like Jenny. She hoped he was right, that he could see further ahead. That her swelling body was on its way to beautiful. With her father around, she felt her soft teenage shape could be a stage to overcome, like acne.

The phone rang again. Before Jenny could reach for it, her mother rose and picked up the receiver. "Hello?" she said, and waited. "No thank you, we're not interested at this time."

Jenny looked across the table at Sam, *at this time*.

He mouthed, "Pants on fire."

"Someone selling garden hoses of all things," her mother said, carrying over a bowl of fruit salad for dessert. The patio was still wet from where she'd dragged their hose from pot to pot to douse her herbs and strawberries that afternoon. Alibi, Jenny thought, but not alibi. Liar.

"Garden hoses," her father said. "What an idiot."

Her mother looked down at the brown noodles she was catching with her fork.

"He cares about plants," Jenny said.

"Saving the petunias," her father said, and nodded. "Honorable."

"I don't believe making money off the needs of another guy's flowers is honorable," Sam said, and Jenny kicked him under the table. He kicked her back, his sneaker scraping her bare ankle, but she didn't flinch.

Her father winked at Sam, then looked at Jenny.

"What do you think, Jen? Isn't that commerce?"

"Just as easy to go to the store than have it sent to the house and not know what you're getting," Jenny said.

Her mother sat back from the chow mein and sipped her wine.

"It's about convenience," her mother said.

Sam faked a sneeze into his napkin. He wanted Jenny to look at him. He wanted both of them to turn hysterical.

"Are you getting sick, too?" her mother said to Sam.

"Maybe," Sam said.

"I like going to the store," Jenny said.

"I agree with Jen," her father said. His eyes twinkled. He had twinkling eyes, her father, and he loved roller coasters. They rode in the front car and never held on to the safety rail. Put your arms up in the air, he would say, and scream.

She could've asked her father for the car, but then he'd ask her mother, and her mother would never have agreed. Her mother worked against extravagance in children. And if her father had to choose between Jenny and her mother, he would choose her mother. He would choose her mother over everybody.

*   *   *

The next day Jenny went to school. When she got home from band practice, her mother was *at a movie with Barbara from down the street* and her father was watching the Dodgers on TV. Sam was out playing Dungeons & Dragons with some kids from Developing Economies. Jenny made popcorn for her father. On TV, a Dodger walked up to the plate, kicked the dirt, and cranked his bat up behind his shoulder.

From the couch, her father said, "Swing for the fences."

Last summer her mother threw a surprise party for her father's fortieth birthday. She hung paper lanterns from the magnolia tree in the yard. She set up round tables with white cloths and a bartender on the patio. She wore a silver wrap dress that tied at the hip, plunged at the neckline, and slit up the side to show most of her thigh. While they waited for Sam to show up with her father, her mother introduced Jenny to guests. She held Jenny's hand and pulled her around like a prop, a toddler's ugly wooden duck tied to a string. Or not a duck, a blue elephant. In her blue cotton dress with red polka dots. "This is my beautiful daughter, Jennifer," her mother said over and over. Jenny stood there and smiled while the guests praised her mother for her shimmery dress, her whimsical lanterns. Jenny felt like a bystander to her own existence. Her mother quickly bored of their charade and left her by the hedge with a hook-nosed woman talking about time-shares on Kauai. Sam and her father arrived and everyone yelled, *Surprise!* When her father opened his arms to the crowd with what Jenny supposed was astonishment, her mother dove into them and he hugged her until her painted toes lifted up from the grass. Her mother's audience erupted in hoots and hollers and thundering applause.

✳   ✳   ✳

The morning of Jenny's birthday, there was no Scirocco parked in the driveway. On the walk to the bus stop, Sam picked a weed flower from the scrub grass along the sidewalk. He handed it to Jenny, and she tucked the yellow flower behind her ear.

"You can't blackmail someone if you're not prepared to go through with it," Sam said.

"Is that your pathetic way of asking if I'm going to tell Dad?" Jenny said.

"You won't," Sam said. He wore his backpack on both shoulders. Jenny couldn't stand his maturity.

"I only just woke up," Jenny said. "The day is long."

Alas, long with disappointment. She had thought the car would be there; she had believed in her car, in the red bow tied around its hood. She had believed in her parents, her mother and her father. They would do the right thing. But that morning she stared out her bedroom window at the empty driveway, willing the Scirocco to her, prying it loose from the car dealership with her magnetic thoughts. When the driveway remained blank, she hated its cement, the crack down its middle, the basketball hoop crooked above the garage door.

"Then act like you mean it," Sam said.

"I do mean it," she said. She'd followed his directions, taped pictures of Sciroccos inside her mother's makeup drawer, her jewelry drawer, her purse, her stash of chocolate nonpareils hidden in the rice cooker.

"Turn up the heat," Sam said. "That's all I'm saying."

Jenny thought of bacon sizzling in a pan. She wanted to be the stove burner, or the pan. She was the bacon.

She took her driving test that afternoon in the Volvo.

"Nonetheless," her mother said into the car on the way home. They had not spoken since Jenny had finished her test, refused to smile for her license photo, and discovered her mother leaning against the Volvo in the parking lot with a lit cigarette. Lucky Strikes. Jenny had never seen her mother smoke. She walked right past her mother and slid into the driver's seat.

As Jenny drove, her mother fiddled with the latch on her purse. "I'm going to bake your cake, angel food with whipped cream and strawberries," she said. "Drop me at home and you can drive to the market for cream and berries. Your inaugural flight, to Safeway."

Jenny held the steering wheel at ten and two o'clock and checked her rearview mirror every five seconds. "Is Federico from Spain?" she said.

Her mother rolled down her window and lit another cigarette. She held the cigarette casually out the window and blew smoke sideways from her mouth so it caught the wind.

"I don't want to talk about Federico."

"Federico sounds Spanish," Jenny said.

Her mother stubbed out the barely smoked cigarette against the Volvo's door and dropped it into the road. *Littering*, Jenny thought.

"He's from Argentina," her mother said. Her mother blinked at the palm trees bending over the road, their sunbaked fronds brown and curled. "But that doesn't matter."

Jenny watched the painted dashes in the middle of the road, kept to her side. The asphalt glinted in the sunlight. Up ahead, the light at the intersection turned yellow, and she gently pressed down on the brake.

"Where's my car?" she said.

Jenny stopped at the red light and looked at her mother.

"Your *car*?" Her mother's eyes widened like in a cartoon. "I'm trying to find my happiness, can't you see?" Her mother did not look pretty with her eyes round and her chapped lips pulled back against what Jenny could see were yellowing teeth.

The light turned green and Jenny drove. She kept her eyes on the road, her hands on the wheel. Jenny thought she must not care about her mother's happiness, because she couldn't bear to hear her mother speak of it.

When they got home, her mother came around to where Jenny stood on the driver's side. She set her purse on the hood of the Volvo. Here it is, Jenny thought, *the standoff*.

"I won't be blackmailed, Jennifer."

"Then you should've gone to a hotel."

Her mother's small hand flew out high and hard and slapped her cheek. Jenny smelled her mother's perfume in the sting on her skin.

"Federico is a friend of your father's." Her mother's face winced at the lie or the hitting, Jenny couldn't tell. "He's worried about your father, that's why he was here."

Jenny held her cheek. Her eyes filled with water.

"That doesn't explain anything."

"To me, it does," her mother said.

"You still have a husband *and* a Federico," Jenny said, and scooted into the house before her mother could slap her twice.

❋   ❋   ❋

Jenny told Sam that Federico was not a Spaniard or an Italian. He said, "In Argentina, adultery is ubiquitous." Instead of asking what Sam meant by *ubiquitous*, Jenny went to her room. She found the cat sleeping in a square of sunlight on the floor. She curled her body tightly around him and made herself small. The sun was warm on her back, and the cat began to purr. Jenny pressed her reddened cheek into the carpet and felt a prickly burn.

When the light moved away from them and the room dimmed, Jenny took Mr. T outside to lie on the hammock under the magnolia tree. In the kitchen, she passed her mother mixing lemonade in a pitcher. On hot days, her father liked a glass of her mother's lemonade spiked with vodka from the freezer when he came home from work.

"Sweet sixteen," her mother called out, circling sliced lemons with the spoon. "My first baby, all grown up."

Jenny paused and watched her mother rip mint leaves off their stems and drop the pieces into the pitcher. Her mother dipped the spoon and tasted the lemonade. She was wearing coral lipstick and her hair was brushed. She looked up at the ceiling as if listening for direction from somewhere far away. Then she squeezed another half a lemon over the pitcher, the citrus juice dripping over her fingers and into the lemonade.

"Don't call me baby," Jenny said. "Ever." The cat was heavy. She moved his head up to look over her shoulder. He felt like a baby in her arms.

Her mother wiped her hands on a kitchen towel and went back to mixing her lemonade.

"It was a pretty car you picked out," her mother said.

Jenny held the fat cat and wished Sam were there to say something sharp. Her mind went to the picture of the Scirocco she'd left on her mother's dresser, sun reflecting off the red hood, the silver VW emblem on the front grill. She had been deceived by her wanting, by her faith in a Scirocco. She had believed in magic.

The automatic garage door rumbled, and Jenny and her mother looked at the door where her father would appear. Her mother opened the freezer and pulled out a bottle of vodka. Jenny silently vowed never to speak to her mother again and carried the cat baby outside to the hammock.

✺   ✺   ✺

By the time Jenny has a car, her dead grandmother's Chevy Nova, Sam is gone. He will abandon her for boarding school in Connecticut, his parting words "Every man for himself." She'll never count on him coming back. Her father has already left, moved to a condo in Marina del Rey. He and the other separated husbands were reborn in Marina del Rey. They abandoned their needy children, their pinched wives, for careless stewardesses on layovers at the Marina Hotel. Jenny had seen those fathers turn back into men, with tan, shiny faces and better-fitting clothes. They waited on the sidewalks after school on Fridays, waved heartily to children dragging beneath backpacks and squinting into the sun, then tucked these suddenly quiet boys and girls into their Datsun 280Zs and delivered them into afternoons of pizza and endless quarters at the video arcades. The children visited the condos during these temporary leaves from their broken homes. They regarded the dingy carpeting, track lighting, and black pleather sofa beds with distrust. At night, the sofa beds creaked beneath them. They lay in the dark as boats sloshed water against harbor slips, and they learned that they missed their bedrooms more than they missed their fathers.

Jenny will sleep on the sofa bed in her father's condo only twice. She'll live in this house alone with her mother for what will seem like forever. Her mother will come and go with men who remind her of Federico, though she will never see him again.

But on her sixteenth birthday, Jenny swayed in the hammock and listened to her father whistling at the barbecue. She hated her mother. She hated her mother enough to forget that it was only a car.

Her father painted the birthday dinner steaks with her mother's spicy sauce, then stepped back as the meat sizzled and cackled above the coals. Jenny set the cat on the grass and walked over to her father.

"Dad?"

Her father looked at her from the side, his mouth curling at the edges, expecting a joke.

SMALL IN REAL LIFE

＊　　＊　　＊

*It was a moonlit night, warm and loose, and the party in the Hol-*lywood Hills was taking off. Louis grabbed Roberta's hand and led her past the crowd on Jay's patio toward the house. He had ideas resting on these folks and what they could do for him. What they would do. He felt crackly in his veins. He wanted to come down a little before he mingled, didn't trust himself yet.

Roberta's dress announced an intention. She was a big girl, boned and otherwise, and Louis jived to take her down fast, like a tornado. Tonight he craved impact.

"The actors look small in real life," Roberta said. "Like dolls."

"You're a doll," Louis said. "Come over here."

He pulled her down a hallway in the house. He could've taken her to his room upstairs, with the balcony—"Hey," he had said to Jay, dropping his bag on the plush carpet, "where's the view of the Hollywood sign?" and Jay said, "What are you, a fucking tourist?"—but he wanted to stay closer to the action. So he walked Roberta down the hallway and tried the silver levers on the mahogany doors until he found a bed. There was a black plasma TV on the wall. Obsidian. He smacked Roberta on the ass like she told him to, and she hollered. The music pulsed through the windows. Hip-hop shit. No one could hear them.

His friend Jay had produced the movie. Louis had stayed for the credits: *Produced by Jay Stevens*. Proof.

Louis had found Roberta on the airplane to Los Angeles, walking the aisle in her navy-blue polyester skirt and navy-blue pumps. Fly the Friendly Skies. Yes, he would, thank you. He was on his way to fix things, turn up the heat, embrace the magic. If Jay had made it, there was enough to go around, and Louis headed west with his eyes wide open. Roberta was from Phoenix and based out of Chicago. It was February, but she was brown down through the cleavage. He ordered five rum and Cokes from her so he didn't have to speculate. He said the word *topless* quiet, in his mind, and felt the rise.

* * *

He'd left his wife and baby daughter cooped up in a first-floor apartment in Freehold, New Jersey. He couldn't stand the cloistered scent of family in there together day and night.

"What do you want me to do," his wife had said, "watch porn with you?"

Louis waved her off.

"I wake up to feed the baby and I hear you," she said.

"Hear what?" he said.

"The groans and the sighs and the screwing on TV."

He was a musician. He took pleasure in sound.

"When we were doing it," she said, folding baby shirts into little squares, "I never felt that damn ecstatic."

The circles under his wife's eyes were puffy in the morning, inflated pads marooning her eyelashes, and he wanted to buy her an eye cream. Since the baby, she'd slowed down with her makeup. She wore sweatshirts and pajamas, and she smelled like cheese. The baby smelled like warm flowers, but the baby hadn't rubbed off on her.

She called the baby Bailey, and he said it was a fag's name, or a dog's name, but she didn't listen. He said you can't give a girl that name because people think: fag, boy, *dog*, and then they see the kid's a girl and they're already exhausted by their thoughts. They won't give her a fair shot from the start, he said.

His wife said that if she thought this marriage had a shot, she'd give him a vote on the baby's name, but his dick was loose and his head was tight, and she couldn't see herself getting along with that crowd anymore.

"Then why'd you marry me?" he said.

"I was young and inexperienced," she said.

They'd been married eleven months.

His wife had gorgeous breasts. Soft and plump, they could roll from side to side. He kissed Roberta in Jay's bedroom with the plasma TV and he missed his wife. Or he missed her breasts, but they felt like all of her.

＊　　＊　　＊

Roberta snored, like she'd had a long day up in the air serving plastic trays. Louis left her naked on the bed and walked out to the party. He had imagined Jay in a glass house on the beach in Malibu, but Jay lived in a Spanish number with a red-tiled roof. Sparrows nested in the tiles. They poked their heads over the edge, checked out the drop, and then poked them back in again. There were gold tips on the black iron gates that enclosed the house, and the circular driveway turned around a gurgling fountain. Outside the gates, giant trees with pink and white flowers lined Jay's street, radiating good fortune in the yellow sunlight. Jay pointed at the trees like he'd grown them from seeds. He said, "Magnolias. You ever seen anything as beautiful?"

The trees had polished green leaves, round as saucers. Their delicate petals arched gently into cups. The petals gathered on the fresh-cut grass beneath the trees, soft and pretty like a neighborhood floral arrangement. Jay said the magnolias were from Georgia. They had assimilated like the California eucalyptus—which came from Australia, Jay was a regular arborist—and now everyone thought magnolias were indigenous. Jay liked to say *indigenous* and *assimilated*.

A flagstone path led to Jay's front door. He had a brass knocker that you could kill someone with, if you could rip it off that massive slab of oak. The rooms inside were pure white and the wood floors gleamed; they spun the light like mirrors. In some places, ceilings vaulted high enough for church services. Louis thought of his daughter, when she was old enough, riding a red tricycle across the living room. Whenever he thought about his daughter, she walked and talked and knew he was the best daddy in the world. Because he was always giving her things, like the red tricycle with a bow tied on the handlebars, or a mansion in the Hollywood Hills. He hadn't abandoned her in the apartment in Freehold; he just didn't have anything to do with her the way she was now, squawky and pristine, as if God wanted him to see what he, Louis, could make. Something beautiful, relentless, and unknowable. When he held his daughter in his arms, her soft eyes studied his face with such gonzo admiration he couldn't do it for long. Be in the searchlight of that pure love. His wife complained he never held the baby for more than ten minutes, and he said he worried he was going to hurt her, and he guessed he wasn't good at the baby stuff.

His wife said maybe you wanted a boy so you could play ball. He said no, boys have too much to bear, they got to have strong shoulders, but girls can stay sweet, enjoy themselves, see the sights. His wife pushed aside the venetian blinds on their bedroom window and looked out at the asphalt parking lot and the rain-stained stucco of the apartment building next door. "You're right," she said. "It's gorgeous out there."

Louis went out to Jay's backyard. The pool was lit up in a luscious turquoise. Skinny women in sandals and tank tops, all flesh and iridescence, mixed in with the dark-haired men. He'd never seen whiter teeth or shinier hair. Live mannequins. He couldn't grasp where to start with them.

*   *   *

"Come out for the premiere, Lou. I'm having a party," Jay had said. Jay's whiny voice the same for ten years, bouncing on Louis's nerves.

"I don't know, I've got a gig," he said.

"It's seventy-five degrees outside, man. Get—on—a—plane," Jay said, like Louis was a retard. "I'm wearing a robe and smoking a cigar on my patio. The birds are singing to me. I've got a waterfall that runs right into the pool."

Louis's gig was low-end, not even a gig, backup guitar at a bat mitzvah celebration. The tip was a loaf of challah bread and glassy stares from thirteen-year-olds dressed up in blue eye shadow while he sang backup on a twangy cover of Green Day's "Good Riddance." He hadn't played a bar in years. The old band scattered across New Jersey, and Louis selling AV equipment in a windowless cement box off Route 9. Their band's CDs—the one album—were stacked in neat rows on a shelf in the back of his closet, but he kept a few in the glove compartment. In case he met someone significant, made a connection.

He'd packed twenty CDs in his suitcase for LA.

His wife had sat on their bed and watched him pack. He couldn't catch a whiff of her from where he stood, but he knew the stagnant scent was there. It smudged her features into a blurriness he couldn't see through. She had a set of little scissors and nail files and bottles of polish laid out on a towel beside her.

"Jay's not your friend," she said. She worked a nail file back and forth over her thumb, building a tiny pile of nail dust on the towel.

"I'm not looking for friends," he said.

"Yeah?" She'd say a rude thing like that and not look at him. She examined the cuticle on her pointer finger instead.

"When else am I going to Los Angeles?"

"When Bailey's older."

Louis kneeled in the closet before the box of CDs. He ran his hand over the plastic edges, feeling for the heat of the lucky ones.

"Who knows where we'll be then," he said. He picked out CDs from the top, middle, and back of the box. His luck could be anywhere.

His wife had stopped sawing her nails. She held the little scissors and waved them at him.

"You think you'll be somewhere else? With Jay in Hollywood?"

"What are you saying?" Louis said. He'd thought about that, sure. A leather-paneled recording studio with a fat guy in a Hawaiian shirt working the controls, shifting the treble so Louis's voice came out clear as water.

"Jay calling you doesn't mean shit," she said, as if she knew about his guy in the Hawaiian shirt.

"It means I'm getting out of here."

She picked up a bottle of nail polish, red as blood, and shook it.

"That's what you think," his wife said.

"I'm doing things," he said. "I'm making an effort."

She opened the polish and dipped the brush and painted a dark red stripe across her first fingernail.

"You try in the wrong directions," she said.

❋   ❋   ❋

Louis recognized a police detective from *Law & Order*. There was a woman famous from somewhere else, but he didn't know movie names. Louis tapped the actor from *Law & Order* on the shoulder.

"Hey, officer," he said to the actor, "there's a girl passed out in one of Jay's bedrooms. You wanna have a look?"

The actor looked at him without kindness.

Louis leaned in closer. "She might still be naked," he said. The actor turned back to his group.

"Hey, Lou, whatcha doing that for?" It was Jay. Sneaky as always, pulling on his elbow.

"Doing what?" Louis said.

"Where's your stewardess with the hips?" Jay said.

"What do you mean?"

"You paying her, what's it, by the hour?" Jay said, his eyes squinty.

"You're the guy who pays for it," Louis said.

Jay laughed. "I want to introduce you to someone," he said.

Louis followed Jay to an older man with tan leathery skin and green eyes, dressed up in a jacket and slacks. A lizard in a suit.

"Mel," Jay said to the man, "this is the lead singer of Cosmos, the first band I ever managed. Lou, this is Mel. He scored the music for the movie. He's the best there is and ever was." Jay leaned back on his heels and sniffed, proud like he was standing in front of a barbecue grilling a steak.

Mel looked Louis over, stopping down low at his black monk strap shoes. They were the lucky shoes he wore to gigs, and he'd buffed them with black polish that afternoon. He found them years ago, when the band was still playing, in a store on Broadway in New York; they had every kind of shoe stacked up and down the wall, each one balanced on its own ledge. The buckles on his shoes shined if you had some stage light on them. Mel might've wondered where Louis got his shoes—hell, maybe he had a pair—but when he looked back to Jay while he shook Louis's hand, Louis thought, then again, he might not.

"You were in the business?" Mel said to Jay. "Get out of here."

"I was," Jay said. "I recorded an album for Cosmos. Their one and only. We made these CDs, thousands of them. You should have seen us on the Jersey Shore, man."

"You're from Jersey? I'm from Jersey!" Mel said. He and Jay grabbed arms in a distant, urgent hug. Louis had seen Jay greet other men with the same simulated intimacy. The women he kissed on both cheeks. Roberta liked it. When Louis introduced them, she turned her head after Jay's first kiss as if she knew he'd want the other cheek.

"And I *live* in Jersey," Louis said.

Jay laughed, but Mel still wasn't looking at Louis.

"Have you seen Fredericks, man?" Mel said to Jay. "I gotta find him, tell him about this new project, see if he'll play."

"You looking for guitar, or bass?" Louis said.

Mel looked at him, reptile eyes shifting back and forth.

"Why?" Mel said.

"I play," Louis said. "Whatever you need, I'm your man. Right, Jay? Hell, I brought one of those CDs out for my friend Jay here. We can listen."

The silence lasted long enough for Louis to notice the DJ had changed from hip-hop to retro shit disco.

"We had some good times," Jay said. "We did, Louis."

"Alright, I gotta find Fredericks. I'll see ya," Mel said, and patted Jay on the back and Jay patted Mel, and Mel walked off toward the bartenders.

Jay slapped Louis in the chest. "What are you, an idiot?" Jay said.

"Why'd you introduce me, then?" Louis said.

Jay shook his head like Louis was his kid. Like Louis was *his* kid, when Louis was the one who had let Jay Stevens book their Cosmos gigs and drive the van. They met at Ocean County College, before Louis dropped out. Jay was pale and fleshy with flat brown hair. His sneakers dragged the ground when he walked, as if his limbs lacked muscle, and his throat only had enough to make that reedy voice come out. Louis was spindly and agile. Back then, Louis could stomp and shake on a stage for two sets without a break. The band was so hot it didn't matter who was their manager. Jay harassed Louis with a business proposal, twenty pages typed. "Did you read the proposal, Louis? Did you? Do you have any questions? I've got another copy right here." The guy begged Louis, wore him down like that, until he said yes. He never read Jay's manifesto, but Jay kept the van tuned; he had it repainted charcoal and the windows tinted. He drove up to a club like they were movie stars and he was a real manager. Maybe he was. He was into production from the start. But he'd never be the act.

Louis had the girls then, he had all the girls he wanted. Smart, pretty, dumb, fat ankles, thin ankles, he'd done them right. He would've killed at this party.

"I'm good," Louis told Jay. "You know I'm good."

"I know," he said. Now Jay spiked his hair with gel, looked like he'd put a finger in a socket, and rode a chrome bicycle in his home gym.

"I can play anything," Louis said.

"You *can* play anything," Jay said. He was looking past Louis, at the mannequins. Louis looked, too. They were pressed together in clumps of glossiness on Jay's manicured lawn.

Roberta appeared from the crowd and paused by the side of the pool to sip her drink. She'd lost her shoes and her dress was bunched up and strange, like she'd pulled it on backward.

Louis was going to tell Jay about him and Roberta in the bedroom and the reflection he'd seen of their bodies twisted up together on that plasma TV, but when he turned to his friend, Jay was gone. The sly bastard. Jay invited Louis out to LA to make him feel bad, to show him. And Louis had come along when he called, like a hungry old dog.

"Isn't the pool pretty?" Roberta said when Louis reached her. "I want to go swimming." She tugged at her dress.

"Don't ruin your dress, sweetheart," Louis said.

"Who cares about my dress?" Roberta said. "It's a dress."

Mel stood near them, talking to a young guy wearing a yarn hat striped red, yellow, and green like the Jamaican flag. Fredericks.

"Wait here. I'm going to get my swimsuit," Louis said, and headed to the house.

Louis climbed the stairs to his room and rummaged around in his bag. Then he went out to the balcony and looked down on a magnolia tree. In the moonlight, the budding flowers looked like glowing clams closed around their pearls. Louis held a CD instead of his swimsuit. On the back of every CD case, he had put a gold sticker printed with his name and phone number. Mel would listen, and then Mel would find him.

Louis thought about what could happen. He felt damp under his arms from the possibilities. He would be driving on Sunset Boulevard, his black convertible speeding around the turns and through green lights, coming back from a meeting with Fredericks. They would partner up for Mel's project, write a new song. Like nothing Louis had done before, but he would come up with the bridge on his own and Fredericks would say it was mint. Louis would pull his convertible into the driveway of his house and park under a magnolia. They'd have their own in the front yard. He would walk in the house and hear his music playing, the old band. Out in the yard, his wife and daughter would be eating sandwiches by the pool. His daughter looked like she was five years old, and his wife smiled when she saw him. She said that she was thinking about back home, when it all started, and she wanted to hear his voice, she wanted their daughter to hear her daddy when he was young and crazy. Crazy for you, he would say. Their daughter climbed into his lap and he could feel the sunlight on her perfect skin.

Jay's hacienda had a balcony every ten feet, and on his way down, Louis stopped to look out at the party. He worried Roberta might've jumped in the water, but the pool glimmered its pristine blue. She wasn't lingering by the bartenders, either. Of all the places he could've found her, she was standing with Mel and Fredericks, and Jay. Jay had his arm around Roberta's not-so-slender waist. The place Louis had held on to and appreciated for its docile curve. She was laughing like Jay had said something funny. Then Mel and Fredericks bent their heads together as if they were making plans Louis would want to know about. Roberta turned to Jay and cupped her hand around his ear, whispering a secret.

His wife planned to leave him. He could see that now. She was waiting it out in Freehold until she had a place and some cash, and then she'd be gone. Louis didn't know when she'd started looking back at him as part of the past she'd escape. A check in the mail, a youthful blunder, or nothing. And Jay had asked him to Los Angeles believing he'd never come. Or not thinking about him, just talking, talking, talking Hollywood into the phone. But Louis had shown up with his CDs as though he'd been summoned. Like a fool. Like a desperate bastard. There were no songs with Fredericks. No blooming magnolias. Louis played backup guitar in dingy hotel banquet rooms with foam-paneled ceilings and beige carpet that muffled sound into a dying pulse. He hadn't written a lyric in years. Every morning, he pinned a name tag to his shirt for a low-down hourly wage. His faith was a delusion. No one wanted to hear his voice. It didn't matter what his baby daughter found in his face. She was only a hundred days old.

At first, no one noticed when Louis changed the music. The DJ had slipped away, maybe to the plasma TV guest room. Cosmos wasn't a party band, or a dance band. It was razor-backed and jangly. Louis yelled the lyrics down from the balcony at Jay's collection of actors and actresses and musicians and Roberta, wherever the fuck she was. He didn't see her down there, or Jay or Mel or Fredericks. He wasn't looking anymore. He was singing the tone out of a song he'd scribbled ten years ago on a scrap of paper from the back seat of his junk Honda. His live voice echoed on top of the CD track but wouldn't merge. Jay appeared below the balcony and glared at him, then tried to wave him away, and then laughed like they were in it together. But the glistening, beautiful people glommed together on the lawn like worried fish. They looked at each other and then up at Louis.

The crowds had loved him once. They chanted his name. His wife before she was his wife called herself a Louis groupie. She collected the guitar picks he threw from the stage at the end of a show. The very end, after he'd left the stage and they'd stomped and clapped and hooted for him and he'd come back for that absolute last song. He looked out at his fans, their sweaty, drunk, ecstatic faces, the girls in the front pressing those bodies he wanted close enough to touch, their arms reaching up for him, and he felt humanity, its lust and rapture. That's what his music could do, what it did. He gave people their purity; he shined the crap off their skin, from the jobs and relationships that smeared them up with duty and failure. Louis blew life across at them, and they felt it, they took it in. They flicked their lighters and he could see his fans out there glowing in the dark.

Louis stood on Jay's balcony like this was his finale. He shook his head against the downbeats and closed his eyes as he sang at the moon. His last performance, for the stars in Hollywood.

He curled his body like a discus thrower launching a steel round, and they cowered, some went running. Louis snapped his arm out and flung a CD from the balcony. There were screams as the famous and less-so scurried for cover. The CD landed in the pool and drifted. Jay yelled at him, but the old and young Louis ripped through the next Cosmos song, and Jay's thin lips swung open and closed wordlessly beneath the vocals. Louis worked on his throw. He didn't want a soft splash. He aimed over the green lawn and the shimmering pool, over Jay's bobbing red face, for the waterfall. He tightened every sinewy strand in his arms and legs and then unfurled into the night. Louis splintered the CD and the next and the next, nineteen in all, against the waterfall's sandstone boulders, where the plastic shattered and lay there under the patio lights like shrapnel.

HANDBAG PARADE

*   *   *

On Thursday afternoons, Stephanie and Carol visited their friend Gia. They went every Thursday because Gia had ALS, Lou Gehrig's disease, and though they had nothing to do with it, no one did, they felt guilt by proximity. Gia was their friend, and she was dying of a diabolical disease. Gia, Stephanie, and Carol had met in the agency mailroom when they were just out of college and copying scripts on giant machines in the basement. None of them became agents, or mothers, but for twenty years they'd kept in touch. Gia lived in a bungalow in West Hollywood. Thank God it's one-story, Carol said. Gia used a cane and then a walker, and now the home nurse pushed her around in a wheelchair.

And the hallways are wide, Stephanie said.

But the wheelchair never bothered Stephanie. What bothered her: as of last month, Gia lost her voice. Her body had silenced her. She was alive inside a frozen woman doll, like a Stephen King horror story in reverse. Talk about torture. But no one talked about it. There was a sister in San Diego who tended to things. Stephanie might have been the friend who drifted away near the end, or now, if this wasn't the end, but she couldn't because of Carol. Carol gave her a spine or turned her spineless, she wasn't sure how to look at it.

Stephanie kissed Carol hello on the sidewalk, and Carol turned her left cheek for a kiss, then her right, and her left again like some European. Carol's husband, Phillip, was producing an alien series for Syfy in Croatia. He'd left seven days ago on a ten o'clock flight, which Stephanie knew because she'd dropped him at the airport. Carol thought he'd hired a car. Stephanie waited to feel guilty about Phillip, but instead she felt a tinge resentful toward Carol.

Gia's bungalow was low to the ground and painted a cream color. A patchwork of pink and white pansies bordered the path through Gia's front yard, where once there had been tufts of wild grasses. Gia's sister was a legal secretary who liked to garden. Over the past months, as Gia declined, she'd recast the modern bungalow with suburban charm.

As they headed up the path, Carol passed Stephanie a bag of takeout like she always did so Stephanie wouldn't arrive empty-handed. "Gene-vieve told me the nurse is from the Philippines. We should ask after her family. They had the hurricane." Genevieve was Gia's sister.

"The hurricane was in Puerto Rico."

"Chef Andrés is down there feeding starving people rice and beans. I saw a picture in the paper. He wears a fishing vest with thirty pockets to keep organized."

"In Puerto Rico."

"Okay, Puerto Rico."

Lately, Stephanie considered herself for the people and Carol of them. Carol pushed her black sunglasses higher up her nose. "It's not my fault I was born in Orange County. I'll die out and the world can be a better place."

"You're like pine beetles eating the forests of America, and you'll never die out."

"Maybe that's true, darling, but let's stop the death talk." Carol waved an arm at Gia's house, a stand-in for the dying going on inside.

"You started it."

But Carol couldn't bicker anymore because she was smiling at the young woman waiting on the front porch. Gia's nurse, Esme. Esme had her dark hair tucked into a bun. She wore a blue cotton nurse smock, pants, and running shoes with hot-pink swooshes. A gold cross hung from a thin chain around her neck. She looked fit and capable, like she could take care of paraplegics all week and run a marathon after church on Sunday.

"Hello!" Carol shouted at signs of disease, in this case Esme's nursing smock.

"You're here," Esme said. The jury was out on what Esme thought of Carol and Stephanie, but she and Gia got on. Gia had called her My Angel.

They handed over the bags of takeout and followed her like children to the kitchen. Takeout was Carol's idea of hospitality. She believed Esme would eat the chicken sandwich and stuff one of the green salads into the blender to puree for Gia. Esme put the kettle on for tea. Months ago their Thursday visits had started under the pretense of afternoon tea. Esme explained that Gia couldn't speak, but she could hear and see them. Two blinks "yes," one blink "no." The keyboards and assisted communication devices she'd given up on last week were piled on a side table, waiting for someone to set up again, or throw away.

33

"I love your accent," Carol said to Esme. "Your voice reminds me of the ocean."

"It does," Esme said. She did not think much of Carol.

"Gia must love listening to you."

"You ask her and let me know." Esme could call Carol an asshole like that, and her voice sweetened the words.

"We'll just go back and see her then?" Carol said.

"She's not going anywhere."

Carol frowned, but Stephanie assumed that in Esme's line of work, you cultivated a sense of humor.

In the bedroom, Gia was propped up in bed with pillows, her mouth slightly ajar. Stephanie couldn't help feeling it looked unnatural, as if she were playing a dead body in a student film and soon a fly could crawl across her lips and then lumber out the window. The camera following the fly to the next fated human it encountered. A homeless man packing his grungy blankets and plastic bags into a shopping cart, and from there a mother outside the supermarket wiping melted Popsicle from her toddler son's face. The fly would land on the boy's cheek until the mother brushed it away.

Gia wore a pink scarf around her neck and blush on her cheeks. She blinked twice at them, her blue eyes wet. Her long auburn curls were blown out shiny and straight. Gia had worn her hair loose and springy, but at forty-five she'd become a life-sized My Little Pony. She'd told them dressing up gave her and Esme something to do.

Carol leaned over the bed and kissed her cheek. One cheek for Gia, she was merciful on the dying. Gia didn't move. Stephanie pulled chairs closer to the bed for her and Carol. She took the chair farther away and fiddled with the zipper of her hoodie while Carol went on about the gorgeous weather.

At the agency, Gia, Stephanie, and Carol had delivered scripts wherever they needed to go—studios, production offices, movie sets, hotels, houses, and bedrooms. When Stephanie left, she said driving those scripts around town turned her into a script girl. And though she'd aged out of the term, she still had the same job on set, checking the continuity between takes and the written pages for movies and TV shows. She hustled for work with long breaks in between, stretching her money to last until the next production. She'd gone to sleepaway camp as a kid, and film sets felt like camp. A make-believe place where new friends seemed like best friends and when (not if) she felt loneliness creep into her, she could binge on donuts from the catering tables. She ranked as the least successful among them. Carol married the balding, kindhearted Phillip, a horror movie/alien TV show producer. Instead of having kids, she published coffee table books, the latest about place settings: blue-and-white ceramic bowls for lawn parties, crystal goblets for holiday feasts. But Stephanie had told Phillip that Carol couldn't make you a grilled cheese sandwich if you gave her two slices of American and a sandwich press. Which was true and tacky of her to say. Gia opened her PR firm. Twenty years later, her arms started feeling funny, and soon that was that.

One afternoon when Gia could still speak and Carol was off in another part of the house, she and Stephanie talked about the fatal insides of life: how people forget they're dying twenty-four hours a day until they can smell death in their own bodies. What a shame that was. Stephanie might have slept with Phillip because Gia was dying or because she wanted to or because she was jealous of Carol. She liked Phillip, the way he considered her face when she talked; she felt like a whole person with him. But she wasn't the first woman he'd slept with during his marriage, and she couldn't tell how much she could believe in him.

Gia said if you listen carefully, you can hear death shivering in your veins.

Stephanie had wanted to ask how death tasted, metallic like an iron pill? But Carol came back into the room before she had the chance. They didn't talk death with Carol. She would call them morbid and ruin it.

Carol held Gia's hand. The way she examined Gia's cuticles bothered Stephanie.

"I have good news," Stephanie said. "Phillip gave me a job on his alien show."

One blink from Gia. Stephanie wondered if she knew more than she could say.

"How nice of Phillip," Carol said, and to Gia, "Stephanie's going to Croatia!" She rummaged in her bag until she pulled out a nail file. "When do you leave?"

"Week after next."

"What about that script you were writing?" Carol said.

"It's a good job."

"Yes, it's Phillip's show."

Two blinks from Gia.

Stephanie saluted Gia as if she'd won the point, though she hadn't, not at all. When Carol got the better of her, she'd learned to remove herself to Gia's walk-in closet where clothes hung peacefully and monochromatically, as if color coordination were their purpose. It was only a year ago that Gia still worked with her stylist. At the end of each season, she gave a few pieces to Stephanie, who couldn't afford seasons. Every week Stephanie wore a sweater or jeans or jacket that had belonged to Gia. But Gia held on to her purses. She had drawers filled with them. Each drawer big enough to fit a child, but instead carried Hermès, Prada, Balenciaga, Chanel, Givenchy, Gucci, Louis Vuitton, Bottega Veneta in soft gray pouches.

Stephanie pulled out a purple alligator Hermès. She slid the leather strap over her shoulder and catwalked into the bedroom.

"Someone gave that to her," Carol said, and then to Gia, "Who was it?"

"I can't remember," Stephanie said. She petted the shiny alligator surface. Gia's eyes were cast down, staring into the ivory duvet.

"Can you adjust the pillows for her?"

Carol leaned over the bed and pushed pillows around until Gia looked straight ahead.

Stephanie catwalked in front of the bed, spun around, and then went back the other way. She stuck her knees out and pranced like a model.

Gia blinked twice. Yes.

"Let's see another one!" Carol said.

Next was a soft suede hobo with fringe. Stephanie swung her hips so the fringe fanned out as she strutted past the bed. She paired a red sequined clutch with red stilettos, a standard Louis Vuitton tote with a straw hat for a weekend getaway. For the Chanel flap bag, she took short steps as if she were Carol in a pencil skirt on her way to the podium to accept the selfless-human award for her work on the board of Planned Parenthood.

Carol had turned her chair so she and Gia sat side by side watching the handbag parade. She clapped for every handbag like it was a fashion show. They'd performed for each other while the copiers churned in the agency basement. Impressions of their bosses, the men upstairs shouting into headsets. Then it was bad dates, dumb actor clients, and this was the end, Stephanie supposed. Beautiful purses.

When Stephanie waved a beaded crystal pocketbook, Carol said to Gia, "Didn't you wear that to the Oscars with the vintage Dior?"

Two blinks.

"I'm going to find the picture and show you," Carol said.

Stephanie did not want Gia remembering Dior dresses, Oscars, lunches at Sunset Plaza, or parties at the Chateau Marmont.

"You took the movie director with the webbed hand," she said.

"The webbed what?!" Carol said.

"The movie director with the fingers stuck together," Stephanie said. She stretched her hands out and tried to make her pinkies stick to her ring fingers. "Gia called him Walter Webby."

"That's terrible," Carol said. "Was his name Walter?"

"Carol," Stephanie said. "You're so literal." She fiddled with the ankle strap on the glittery sandals she'd put on for the crystal pocketbook. Gia's Oscar stilettos. They fit her as if they'd come from her own closet.

"I'm trying to remember who it was. What did he direct?"

"I have no idea," Stephanie said. "Gia knows."

"Yes," Carol said. "You know everything about everybody." She kissed Gia's cheek. "I'm going to find that photo. I'll bring it next time."

Carol slathered hand cream on Gia's hands and wrists. Stephanie wished Gia would turn to Carol and yell, "Get your hands off me!"

Stephanie stretched her quad muscle. "I know why I didn't go into this modeling business," she said. "Too much exercise."

"We've had fun," Carol said, "haven't we?"

She rang the Tibetan bell on the nightstand to summon Esme.

Stephanie came out of the closet with a Gucci shoulder bag, an embroidered dragon covering one side. She ran her fingers over the red and yellow stitching, the greens and blues.

"I love this bag," she said.

Esme appeared in the doorway.

"Teatime!" Carol shouted at her nurse's smock.

Esme glided into the bedroom on her sneakers and adjusted the pillows behind Gia. She looked into her face. She waited until Gia blinked twice before she left.

Gia gazed at the wall. Blinking tired her out. Stephanie walked to the end of the bed into her line of sight and dangled the Gucci from her arm.

"One of a kind," she said.

* * *

The next Thursday, Carol was in Croatia. Stephanie arrived at Gia's bungalow with the takeout. Esme took the food and gave her the status report: the same.

"What about her eyesight?" Stephanie said.

"She can see fine," Esme said.

Stephanie pulled a chair to Gia's bedside. Gia wore a navy-blue zip-up sweatshirt, no rouge, and her hair was pulled back into a ponytail. Maybe Esme dressed her up to meet Carol's expectations and down to meet Stephanie's. She was a good judge of character.

Gia's eyes were the same watery blue.

Stephanie was at a loss for conversation without Carol. She worried about Phillip and Carol together in Croatia. She couldn't talk small. She opened the drawer to the nightstand and found a notepad and pencil and a copy of the Holy Bible. Esme must read the Bible to Gia. In her soothing voice, the Bible would be reassuring or horrible depending on the chapter and verse.

Stephanie wrote on a piece of paper from the notepad, *FYI, Gia had a bat mitzvah but she loves bacon.* She left the note poking out of the Bible like a bookmark.

"I left Esme a hint," she said. But there wasn't enough context between her and Gia for humor. That's what Carol provided, another body in the room. Everyone shifted in their seats when a monologue came along. But what choice did she have.

"Carol's visiting Phillip and I've been sleeping with Phillip, so I'm feeling odd about things."

If Gia was listening, she gave no blinks.

"He's been honorable about it, except the part where he's cheating on his wife. Honorable to me. Does that cancel out what he's doing to Carol?"

Gia blinked once.

Stephanie lied and said she had to go to the bathroom. She went to the closet and pulled out the Gucci purse with the embroidered dragon. She traced the dragon scales, the reds, blues, and greens. Then she found the Prada tote and the Balenciaga. She took them into the bathroom where there was a window over the toilet. She stood on the toilet, popped open the screen, and dropped the purses in their soft gray bags into the hedge along the side of the house.

When she returned to the bedroom, Gia's eyes were closed. Stephanie sat in the chair and watched her friend's chest rise and fall with breath, and when it felt like she'd waited long enough, she left, collecting the handbags from behind the hedge on her way out.

❊   ❊   ❊

Stephanie was supposed to be in Croatia the next week, but she arrived at Gia's bungalow as usual. Carol's Range Rover, black and shiny like Darth Vader, was parked in front. Phillip had called Stephanie over the weekend to explain he'd been mistaken. He didn't have a job for her. He apologized and blamed the budget. Stephanie found Carol in the bedroom, filing Gia's nails as if this were any other Thursday.

Gia wore a purple scarf and rouge. She looked good in the princess colors. Stephanie paused in the doorway as if she were intruding, but Carol waved her closer.

"Close the door," Carol whispered.

Stephanie closed the door and pulled a chair over to the bed. The three of them huddled together in Gia's bedroom. Carol was tan from Croatia. She'd let her hair dry naturally and she wore a T-shirt with jeans and sneakers. She was dressed like Stephanie.

"The nurse is stealing," Carol said. "Three handbags are gone."

"What?!" Stephanie said. She didn't have to fake disbelief. It hadn't occurred to her that anyone would notice.

Carol stroked Gia's hand.

"Thank God they didn't take your crystal pocketbook."

Stephanie sat back in the chair.

"How do you know?"

"Her sister called me," Carol said.

Detective Genevieve of the pink and white pansies.

"Which nurse?"

Carol pointed the nail file toward the kitchen. "You know who."

"Esme wouldn't," Stephanie said.

"She did," Carol said. "I never trusted her."

"You liked her voice."

"I lied." Carol eyed Stephanie coolly, then opened the nightstand drawer and pointed at the Bible as if religion were a sign of deviance.

Stephanie's bookmark was gone or buried deep in the New Testament.

"Did you call the police?" Stephanie said.

"The police!" Carol said, and then to Gia, "Sweetie, we'd never call the police." Stephanie closed the nightstand drawer. The Bible made her queasy.

"The last thing she needs," Carol said, "is an investigation."

Gia's mouth slanted open. No blinks. What did she know? Stephanie was a thief.

Carol patted Gia's hand.

"We should be the ones looking after you," Carol said to Gia. "If we were nurses, we would, in a heartbeat."

"I would be a terrible nurse," Stephanie said.

"Not terrible," Carol said.

Stephanie walked into the closet and slung the Louis Vuitton weekend tote over her shoulder as what she wanted was to get out of town for a few days.

"Her sister comes tomorrow to fire Esme."

"Is that okay with Gia?" Stephanie said.

Gia was silent, her blue eyes bright. She could have been thinking about something else entirely. Like when they would leave.

"What else can we do."

She rang the Tibetan bell. Esme carried in their tea on a tray.

"You can leave it on the table," Carol said.

Stephanie felt conspicuous holding the Louis Vuitton tote and set it on the floor.

"Thank you for taking care of Gia," she said.

Esme nodded. "You're welcome." She didn't even glance at Stephanie or the Louis Vuitton. Esme walked over to the bed and looked into Gia's bland face. Stephanie could swear Gia was trying to smile.

HARMONY

*   *   *

If Paul's court-ordered detox had a silver lining, it was the actor in room 21 at Harmony of Malibu, one of the Top Luxury Rehabs of the World. There was a Harmony of Torrey Pines in San Diego and a Harmony of the Redwoods somewhere in Northern California, where Paul assumed redwoods still grew. In Malibu they had famous people, a perk for his boss, Arianna. She was paying for his stint in rehab. "Instead of jail," Arianna said when she'd dropped him off last week. She was wrong. Not instead—until. But that was the other part of Paul's story. Arianna was his girlfriend and his boss, and almost young enough to be his daughter. Or he was almost old enough. He took candid celebrity shots for her blog-rag, *Uncovered*. He was good with narrative, a journalist of the streets: Robertson, Melrose, Rodeo, Sunset Plaza. A stalker and a publicist. Arianna had smuggled a phone into Harmony for him, sewed it like a Girl Scout into the lining of his duffel bag. When he turned on the phone, there was Arianna's text: *SEND PHOTOS OF THE FUCKED-UP AND FAMOUS!*

The actor in room 21 called himself Dennis, a character he played in the horror movie *666 Sixty-Sixth Street*. Dennis saved the actress Raven Wilson from a serial killer knocking off blond girls, chopping their heads off—Paul remembered gruesome spurting plasma—in their largely blond neighborhood. But the serial killer didn't decapitate Raven Wilson because Dennis loved her and protected her from evil.

The actor who played Dennis had been doing rehabs for a decade, and he was alive. Paul submitted this evidence to his counselor, Dr. Small.

"Yes," she said, "a point in your favor." The point of rehab was to compare yourself to the other shitheads. You were better if they were worse. "But how will this time be different?"

They faced each other in cozy beige chairs in her office. Through the picture window, a gray line of hazy ocean marked the horizon.

Dr. Small took off her running shoes and sat cross-legged. Paul did the same. He was getting flexible. Every morning he lay in bed waiting for Yoga by the Sea, six-thirty to seven-forty-five a.m. His knees didn't even splay out when he sat with his legs crossed like Dr. Small. Paul respected her pale cheeks and the fractured red veins around her nostrils; even the gray hair at her temples had an effect on him. He'd never come across a woman in Los Angeles aging by nature.

"It's only my second time," Paul said.

"You can keep coming back, until you die."

"Addiction is a disease."

"You develop better habits, or you die." Dr. Small wiggled her toes.

He rolled up his sleeves and showed her the white insides of his arms. "I don't shoot up."

"Low bar," she said.

Dr. Small called Paul a professional photographer on a self-inflicted detour. If he were shooting Dr. Small in the studio, he would need the softest light. He would pinch her cheeks for color and use ChapStick on the dry grooves in her lips. But he worked doorsteps, lobbies, airports, hotel hallways, coffee shops, and the sidewalks outside restaurants, gyms, yoga studios, and hair salons; once, he hung out of a helicopter with a telephoto for a Santa Barbara wedding. He used light to peg his subjects to a brief, limited truth: scooting through LAX with hair flattened and eyes baggy from the red-eye, staggering out of a club with their married co-star's hand in their jeans, slinking through the underground parking lot of the plastic surgeon's office building.

"What do you want, Paul?"

"I'd like to go back to seventh grade and not take that beer Trey Garrity stole from the fridge in his garage."

Dr. Small sighed. "Thirty years later, Trey Garrity."

"No," he said. "Lack of willpower."

"We can help you develop the habits you need for that," she said. "The smallest start is a beginning." She recited a Harmony mantra. If he'd ever held Dr. Small's attention, he'd lost it. Not that he had any interest in her, either. He was over her nature-over-culture rebellion. Her hairy thatch.

"I feel that," Paul said. "I feel it all the way down to my toes."

"Okay," she said, and smiled as if he were an ignorant child.

Paul put on his shoes and found his lawyer downstairs in the Family Meeting Room, like this was a reunion. The lawyer wore blue suits and white shirts, never a tie. He had dark, round eyes of admonishment. Arianna had hired him. She called him *the best there is*. The lawyer opened his briefcase and pulled out a yellow legal notepad. There were little bottles of water lined up on the side table. The lawyer cracked open a water bottle, fitted his thick lips around the opening. Hydrated, he started with the usual:

How many drinks? Liquor, wine, beer? Why did you think you could drive? What was the weather like? When had it last rained? Were the roads dry? When did you last have the car serviced? What do you remember? The tree? The smashed windshield? Who pulled you out of the car? What was the extent of your injuries? Who told you about the kid? How did you feel when they told you?

I don't know. Yes, yes, yes. I always drive. Night. I don't know. I don't remember. I don't know. Not much. No. No. A fireman. Scratches. A policeman. Surprised.

"Sad," the lawyer said. "You felt sad."

"Right."

"Shocked, sad, devastated," the lawyer said.

"Yes."

"You're going to take a plea. I'd say seven years and out in five." The lawyer scribbled an illegible sentence on his legal pad. "You're not sympathetic."

"I'm a white male."

"You're an alcoholic."

"In treatment."

"Who cares," the lawyer said. He handed Paul a business card and closed up his briefcase. He always handed Paul a business card at the end of their meetings. To Paul, it meant the lawyer was leaving, not that he could be reached.

"The kid was twenty-four," the lawyer said.

"He was a photographer," Paul said, "like me."

"That's nice," the lawyer said. "I bet he was talented."

"He was."

"When you and I are dead," the lawyer said, "we can be talented."

✳   ✳   ✳

Camera ready, here comes Dennis.

Paul clicked the button over and over on the camera phone he held in the upstairs window and guessed at Arianna's caption: *[Dennis] saunters across the Harmony lawns in leather sandals.* She was in her heart a failed poet. Online, a former *Us Weekly* intern.

Out there on the green grass, Dennis's linen pants and shirt billowed, his dark hair ruffled in the ocean breeze. He was short like an actor. *He's one of the idiots*, Arianna would text when she blew up Paul's photos (and video!). Paul loved his boss/girlfriend for seeing through the sheen. Dennis was basic handsome, a high school prom king from a mediocre town, say Seal Beach. But he had enough luck to marry Raven, now an A-list actress and a brunette. She visited him at Harmony, wearing a scarf over her head and large black sunglasses.

Ah, Brigitte Bardot, Arianna would text. And Paul would respond, *No, Audrey Hepburn.*

It was time for Group. Paul hid the phone in the secret Girl Scout pouch in his duffel. He had the feeling their rooms were searched. They said so in the Harmony pamphlet, under *Security*, as if violating your privacy could resolve your addiction.

Dr. Small waited alone in a circle of folding chairs while the Groupies crowded a cookie tray and pitcher of lemonade. They were as young as their afternoon snack: wispy hair, torn concert T-shirts, multiple ear piercings, low-riding pants. Fans of heroin and oxy, they showed up in LA for creative impulses that hadn't panned out, yet. They populated their own subculture of not making it, time and money for using, for yard parties with B- and C-listers in Echo Park. Spineless parents dropped these kids off at Harmony, signed the papers, cried into wads of tissue, and then drove away in rental cars.

"Youth today," Paul said to Dr. Small. And then, because he couldn't resist, it would be the end of him, that he couldn't resist—it made him good at his job and nothing else—because of that, he leaned closer to Dr. Small.

"Why did Raven Wilson visit our guy Dennis in rehab when she's married to that TV actor?"

It bothered Paul, their collective acquiescence. Dennis's celebrity marriage meant he played pretend while the rest of them lay bare their truest and ugliest secrets as mandated for this resurrection of the soul.

Dr. Small curled her chapped lips over her teeth and shook her head like she'd walked into a room and found a terrible mess.

"You have plenty of your own business to mind," Dr. Small said. "Leave him alone."

She was onto him. He felt a mild surprise at not caring if she considered him despicable, a fleeting sense of his own disaffection, whereas before rehab he would have felt nothing at all. Dr. Small had achieved a blip in what she called their work together, her work and his court-mandated attendance. Or the fleeting sense came, like his opening hips, from Yoga by the Sea.

The purpose of Group was to describe a moment you were psychologically eviscerated to eight strangers sitting on metal folding chairs. Today, a skinny musician with one Grammy-nominated song talked about her boyfriend stealing money from her. *She's last year [thumbs-down emoji]*, Arianna had texted back to his picture of the skinny musician biting her nails. But the skinny musician had played her electro-pop-folk music at the MTV Video Music Awards. *Also last year [poison-skull-head emoji]*. Paul called the girl the Fifi Lapel of the twenty-teens. Who's Fifi Lapel? the skinny musician had asked. He told her Fifi Lapel had gone out with Oscar-winning director George Andrew Sorenson, who was now married to the actress Gillian Delacourte—they had a freaky number of kids, even a gender-reconsidered girl-boy—and then Fifi went out with someone else, but he couldn't remember who.

"Why does that matter?" the skinny musician had said.

"That's the point," Paul said. "It doesn't matter anymore."

The skinny musician spoke softly, and the rest of them leaned into the circle. Their chairs creaked under the weight. Her boyfriend had slipped her ATM card out of her wallet, withdrew a thousand dollars from her account, and put the card back before she noticed. She went to the bank about the mysterious weekly withdrawals, and they said it's the boyfriend, it's always the boyfriend. But she didn't believe them. She thought it was a computer error, a digital glitch in cyberspace, until the morning she walked in on her boyfriend taking her ATM card from her wallet. The skinny musician sniffled, wiped her nose with the back of her hand, and stared at the beige rug. Everyone leaned back; the chairs creaked. Dennis raised his hand, and Dr. Small nodded. Dennis said he related to the skinny musician's trust issues. He said, given the nature of his career, he couldn't have real friends. He couldn't trust anybody. Dr. Small said Dennis and the skinny musician with the thief boyfriend didn't have the same trust issue. They were just tangentially related in the inherent loneliness created by their situations. Yes, Dennis said, I feel inherent loneliness. He looked down at his hands in his lap. Paul could've looked away, but the hipsters were staring at Dennis, so what's one more pair of eyes.

After Group, Paul and Dennis sat on the green Adirondack chairs and watched the ocean rolling into the cliffs below. Most of rehab was sitting in chairs. They smoked, tipping their ashes onto the grass.

Dennis said if he'd known what it would be like being famous, he would've been a furniture maker instead.

"Furniture makers have real friends," Paul said.

"The fuck right they do."

"Would you live in Greensboro, North Carolina?" Paul had read an article about furniture makers in Greensboro. They chopped their own wood in a Carolina forest.

"Maybe. I'd have a house and a wife. I'd make all the furniture, the kitchen table, the bed, the nightstands, bunk beds for our kids. Maple, everything in maple."

Dennis's wife, Raven, lived in a house on the beach. In Group, he called his wife Cassandra. Early in her career, she'd made a guest appearance as Cassandra, the brain tumor patient on *Palo Alto Hospital*. This was Paul's online research. The *Palo Alto* doctors performed an experimental surgery and called her recovery a miracle.

"You have a house and a wife."

"But not the furniture," Dennis said. He looked down at his burning cigarette.

"Summers are hot in North Carolina," Paul said.

"I wouldn't have to live there," Dennis said. "What I'm talking about is building with your hands, a sensual, daily practice."

"Like sex, in hardwood."

"Yes!" Dennis put out his fist for a bump. Paul bumped fists with Dennis.

Dennis exhaled a ring of smoke, and Paul exhaled a ring of smoke right after. The smoke rings roped around each other as they drifted.

"This is as close to real as it gets," Dennis said.

"Amen, brother." Paul lit another two cigarettes and handed one to Dennis. They say people have individual neurons in their brains that light up when they look at a celebrity. Each celebrity has their own neuron in your head. Paul watched Dennis gaze at the sunset and waited for his neuron to go off.

Nothing.

He sent Arianna the video of Dennis walking across the lawn. She texted back the emoji with an X over one eye and the tongue out. It could be Dennis after they were through with him, or her feelings about Paul's so-so information, or a stand-in for Paul locked up with the likes of Dennis for the month. With Arianna, he didn't know how to interpret every emoji.

He had a message from his lawyer: *Let's not push your luck too far. Call me ASAP.*

Paul didn't call back. Who would? It smelled like a bad deal.

At night, he lay in bed listening to the ocean until the skinny musician tapped on his door with her bitten-down fingernails. Then they screwed, and Paul held her and she cried. One night after she stopped crying, they opened the shade and looked at the moon shining down on the black ocean.

"Do you believe in God?" he said.

"Uh-huh," said the skinny musician.

"I turned a man into a saint."

"You're like God, then." She found her T-shirt in the covers and pulled it over her perfect little Fifi Lapel head.

"I'm his disciple," Paul said.

*   *   *

After another week of clean blood draws and small talk with Dr. Small, she clipped an ankle monitor around Paul's leg. She drew a circle on a Google Maps printout, with the Harmony castle as the red Google teardrop in its center. He could drive five minutes to the Starbucks across the highway from the surfer beach in Trancas. Paul had asked for privileges, but it was a letdown. He didn't feel improved. His right hand had a tremor that came and went, an electrical fault somewhere inside, shaking itself out through his fingers. Dr. Small said the tremor was just the beginning. Of what she didn't name. And he couldn't drive. They'd taken his license the night of the accident.

Dennis had off-campus privileges and a car. That afternoon, they walked through the field of palm trees, the Trees of Reflection, to the residents' parking lot. Dennis clicked the black square of the car key. The brake lights of a blue Toyota Camry blinked from the third row.

"My assistant's car," Dennis said. "Camouflage."

"What's she driving?"

"My Porsche." Dennis laughed. His linen pants hid the ankle bracelet. Paul's pant leg caught up on his ankle band, pulled down his jeans at the waist. The ankle monitors were for special situations. Like vehicular manslaughter or, in Dennis's case, court-ordered rehab for possession.

Dennis slid open the sunroof, and they coasted down the hill, away from Harmony. He rolled down the windows and dialed up Frank Sinatra. "Fly Me to the Moon." Once they passed through the gates, Dennis straightened his elbows and gripped the steering wheel and accelerated into the curves. He'd raced cars for Pennzoil in the movie *Formula One,* his last on the big screen and memorable, it appeared, to him. Paul held on to the door handle. He didn't think they'd go over the guardrail into the ravine, but in the speeding Camry with Dennis's hair flapping and his white linen outfit rippling in the wind and Sinatra's croony lyrics in stereo, the guy was an escapee from the asylum as far as Paul could tell.

At the coast highway, Dennis slowed for a stoplight.

"When we get out of the car," he said, "don't talk to anyone."

Paul gave him a thumbs-up. His hand jerked with the tremor, and his thumb flicked out like he was hitching a ride.

Dennis eyed the dangling thumb and then the ocean across the road, the surfers in black wet suits on their boards, rising and falling with the swells.

"They'll say it means your liver's wrecked," Dennis said. "So don't listen to *them.*"

"It's nothing," Paul said.

"You know how if you cut the arm off a starfish, the starfish grows back the arm?"

"Yes."

"That's the liver," Dennis said. "The liver rejuvenates."

"Regenerates."

"That's what I said."

Starbucks was on one side of a grocery store parking lot. Dennis parked at the end of a line of Harley motorcycles. He looked over the Starbucks patio, at the bearded bikers in black leather vests, the surfers in board shorts and flip-flops, the teenage girls in halter tops. "Casting call, Malibu," he said.

Then he pushed his sunglasses higher up the bridge of his nose and checked his tousled hair in the rearview mirror.

"Do not talk to anyone," Dennis said. "I repeat, don't talk to anyone."

If Paul had been paying attention, he would've noticed the girl in the aviators, the phone in her hand, how she tilted it slightly and pouted as if for a selfie. He relied on tipsters: valets, hairstylists, waiters, bodyguards, production assistants, doormen. Yes, he could say to the judge about the night the kid had died, I received a tip and was en route to the Peninsula Hotel. I didn't intend to speed. [Pause.] But I suppose I was in a hurry. My livelihood depends on getting the first shot.

He followed Dennis inside Starbucks. They bought iced cappuccinos, triples. It took five minutes, maybe ten, before they picked up their drinks from the counter. It wasn't enough time, but it must've been because as Paul followed Dennis out the doors into the sunlight, he heard the clicks—two Canons and a Nikon. Dennis crouched and turned his back to them instantly. Three men in dark T-shirts and faded jeans lifted and lowered the cameras, pushed in on them. Clicking and shouting for Dennis in his real name. For a second Paul didn't understand who they were calling for. Dennis stayed low and grabbed Paul's arm, pulled him close as if to protect him. Paul felt a pang of relief, of safety. Then Dennis swerved away from the Starbucks doors. He gripped Paul's other arm, dug his fingers into the skin, and shoved Paul backward into the cameras. Paul flailed as he fell, his wrist smacking two lenses. The paparazzi yelled, "Hey, watch out, asshole," and recoiled, lifted their precious cameras above their heads as Paul hit the pavement. His iced cappuccino smacked the ground beside him. He watched the men's dirty tennis shoes as they turned and ran from him. They called after Dennis, who fled across the parking lot to the Camry, his sandals slapping the asphalt.

From the Starbucks patio, Paul watched Dennis climb into the Camry and speed out of the parking lot, the paparazzi firing their cameras at his back. They were Hail Mary shots. Worthless. He'd gotten away.

The girl in the aviators sat at her table, her phone sideways, scanning the scene on video. She paused on Paul. He gave her the finger. She put down the phone.

"What's your name?" she said.

"Warren Beatty."

She typed into her phone, and then he heard the swoosh of her email. She'd sent the video. Another five hundred dollars for the tipster.

Dr. Small picked him up in a minivan.

"Dennis is not a safe friend for you."

"It wasn't his fault."

"That's what everyone says about Dennis," Dr. Small said.

"They came after him." At Harmony, they expected you not to behave like yourself. So Paul got thrown down; he'd done plenty of throwing. Next time he'd have his eyes open.

"Excuses," Dr. Small said.

"What if the excuse is what happened?"

"It's still an excuse," she said, which reminded him not to give Dr. Small more credit than she deserved.

She flicked on her blinker, and they turned into the front gates. Harmony's brown tiled roof and creamy stucco walls rose before them. A few of the twenty-year-olds flung a Frisbee back and forth across the lawn. Between throws, they stood still, hunched over, waiting.

"Did he come back?" Paul said.

Dr. Small pulled up in front of the entrance and waited for Paul to get out. He could've been a hotel guest returning from a day trip to the Mayan temples.

"Dennis always comes back."

❋ ❋ ❋

WTF?! WTF Warren Beatty?! Arianna's text.

❋ ❋ ❋

Dennis showed up at the Adirondack chairs after dinner. They smoked as the sun fell into the ocean and the sky turned pale blue.

"I'm leaving day after tomorrow," Dennis said. "I've got a movie in Vancouver. Cassandra's coming with me. I play a hit man with a conscience."

"Troubled villain," Paul said. "I can see it."

"I can't fuck up," Dennis said. "The movie, Cassandra, none of it. Nine lives, man, I ran them through."

"You don't have to apologize," Paul said.

"It's my last chance," Dennis said.

"You got ten lives," Paul said. "Fuck 'em."

"Yeah," Dennis said, taking another drag on his cigarette. "Fuck 'em."

"Why'd you throw me at the cameras?" Because I don't give a shit about you either is what Paul was saying.

Dennis, for his idiocy, comprehended the language of men. He smiled a movie-star smile, like in the third act of the movie, when they hold on the actor whose eyes sparkle with mischief and, just beneath that, their understanding of their unassailable popularity.

"Instinct."

That night the skinny musician didn't cry afterward. She was feeling better. She'd made plans to stay with her parents in Colorado for the summer. Paul said Colorado was for horses, not skinny musicians. She rolled off him and sat up naked in his bed.

"Our relationship is destructive."

"Who says it's a relationship," Paul said. "Dr. Small?"

"I don't want you to drag me down," she said.

"Is this your higher power talking?" They each had a higher power. They were encouraged to speak its truths. Paul's higher power was an eagle roosting in the center of his forehead, squatting in the middle of his third eye. Nesting there, digging its talons into his brain. Dr. Small should meet his eagle, its badass baldness.

The skinny musician gathered her clothes and left.

Silence, they also learned in Group, can kill you.

Paul got up and looked out the window. The moon was gone. The ocean invisible, waves smashing against the beach one after the other, over and over. Relentless and the rest of it. He assumed jail didn't look like it did in the movies. Polished cement floors and smooth, painted gray bars and metal beds with striped mattresses and pillows. He was guilty on the facts: they had the blood test, the witnesses, the dead kid. He'd written a letter to the kid's parents in Fresno. He'd written about what a great person the kid was even though he didn't know the kid's last name. They'd met a few weeks before outside the Whiskey, waiting on a tip about a top-tier star on a bender. Paul had written about being in the wrong place at the wrong time. He wasn't sure if that had been meeting the kid at the Whiskey that night or the kid saying yes when he offered him a ride two weeks later. There was no tip about the Peninsula Hotel. He and the kid were going for a drink after work; he'd said, Let's get a drink and I'll teach you the panties shot. The kid said, You mean their crotches, their cunts? Paul meant panties. He drove fast around the corners, getting those other words out of his head. Sure, he was drunk, too. That wasn't a contributing factor, though, that was his equilibrium. Excuses, Dr. Small would say.

He'd thrown away the letter. Then he went back to the trash and pulled it out and lit it on fire with a match. Arianna was honking outside his apartment; she was driving him out to Harmony. She was dressed up in her black entertainment pantsuit with stilettos. A hooker of the interweb. He supposed he did what she told him to do because he loved her.

*　　*　　*

The lawyer called again, and they found him in his room, lying on his bed with his eyes closed but not sleeping. The tremor shook all his fingers now; he considered the spasms crawling up his arm like gangrene, and then his shoulder, and from there his heart or his brain. He lay there with his eyes closed, trying to get a sense which way they would go. Brain. Heart.

The lawyer said he liked to deliver this kind of news in person, but the traffic was insane. The lawyer told Paul he did the best he could, which is all any of us can do in this life. Then Paul called Arianna.

"Take the deal, baby," she said. "I'll be here when you get out."

Five years, not a chance.

"Marry me."

"Why?"

"Conjugal visits."

"What?"

"We love each other," Paul said.

"Yes," she said. "I do, baby, I really do."

He didn't ask again.

Paul and Dennis snuck out past curfew. Harmony had twenty-four-hour video surveillance, but no security. He imagined Dr. Small watching the footage each morning with her mug of chai latte. Dennis brought a weed brownie. One of the cooks had hooked him up that afternoon.

"It doesn't sound like a deal," Dennis said. "Penalty. Plea penalty."

Paul's head felt light. The brownie was getting to him. He smelled the particles of salt in the sea air.

"I'll get a job," Paul said. "I'll smuggle shivs through the laundry."

Dennis laughed. Paul couldn't see his handsome eyebrows, his brown doe eyes, or his megawatt smile, but there they were in the warm pitch of Dennis's voice. Their stardom a permanent blessing. Dennis didn't keep coming back to Harmony because he failed; he came back because he and his inherent loneliness would survive.

Dennis let the laugh die out into a hearty chuckle and then into nothing.

"You could do worse," he said.

"Worse than prison?"

"Shit," Dennis said. "I guess not."

He braced his hands against the Adirondack and stood up.

"Good luck, man," he said. "I'll pray for you. You've been a friend."

"I hope so," Paul said.

Dennis put his hand out. Paul reached forward and willed the shake out of his fingers, his thumb, but it was there, and Dennis held strong till the shaking had nowhere to go and then pulled Paul into his chest, and they hugged, and it was a real warmth hugging Dennis, a human embrace. Paul believed in those few seconds his liver could rejuvenate and regenerate. Dennis clapped Paul twice on the back and stepped away into the dark, back to his room, where he would pack and sleep and leave in the morning for Vancouver with his Audrey Hepburn wife.

Paul was not lonely or desperate later that night when he cruised the hallway in his socks, slid on the wood floors like an ice-skater taking strokes, until he reached the skinny musician's door and found it unlocked. He was stoned and horny when he stepped into the dimly lit room, a forbidden candle flickering on the nightstand, jazz playing on the Harmony-issued Bang & Olufsen stereo, and on the bed, Dennis's white butt thrusting in the air. It was a miracle, Paul believed, that he had his phone in his pocket, that he remembered to turn off the flash, that a lavender-scented candle (as he smelled it) cast enough light to make out naked Dennis and the skinny musician, their eyes closed in concentration or elation or embarrassment, he could not tell then or later from the photos, and that they did not hear him.

Dr. Small was right: he was a professional.

❋   ❋   ❋

Paul worked the DENNIS file all night. He typed into his tiny phone the bit about Raven's alias, Cassandra, and the new movie in Vancouver. The part about Dennis using up his nine lives. The marijuana brownie and the skinny musician and the alleged sex addiction.

Paul listened for the ocean below the cliffs, churning in the dark. He thought he could hear the suck and thrust of the water. He would go to prison. He would teach a photojournalism class to men with tattoos and beards and shorn heads. He would teach them how to work the sidewalk outside a nightclub. How to go down on one knee and angle the camera up when a car pulls to the curb. As the car door opens, he would say, you're already shooting, your finger on the button over and over because the girl will rush, she will swing her legs around, and when she stands, she can't keep her knees together, and that's the second you want, the cunt shot.

I named it after a talented friend of mine.

In the morning, Raven drove up the hill to Harmony in the Porsche. She parked in front and walked around the car to lean against the passenger door. Paul took a picture from his bathroom window. She wore the scarf and the sunglasses and a pink silk dress—*diaphanous*, Arianna would say in the caption, this photo next to the other, last night's sex shot. Everything is a story. Dennis walked out in jeans and a tight T-shirt, his biceps cut and tanned as if they'd been gestating in the billowing white linen. Raven squealed and lifted her sunglasses and kissed him on the mouth. Dennis reached for her thigh, his hand slipping beneath her dress, and Paul clicked the camera phone as fast as he could.

RED BLUFF

❋ ❋ ❋

At the end of a blistering July, Tessa Dean snuck out of Camp Weyamucca with her best friend, Barrett Winslow. It was 1974 and Barrett said they had better things to do than float a canoe across the lake or shoot an arrow at a bull's-eye nailed to a stack of hay. The girls were almost fourteen years old.

The path through the forest was black and cold and smelled of dirty pine needles. Barrett hated the smell and Tessa the dark. They wore Tretorns and tennis socks with little white pom-poms attached at the back, above the heel. They had been best friends for three years and went from school to camp together and back to school. They had crushes on different ninth-grade boys. Barrett's was blond with green eyes like hers, and Tessa's wore wire-rimmed glasses. She didn't wear glasses, but she was known as studious and careful. She had long, flat dark brown hair and a librarian face, round and neutral, as reported by every mirror she'd looked into, hoping for more than the plain nose and almond eyes gazing back at her.

They headed away from the lake toward the road. Barrett held the flashlight, went first. Night was cold in the mountains, the crisp air settled around the lake as if the sun's dry summer heat might never come again. Twigs and pine needles crunched under their steps. Tessa listened hard for bears. Once she heard wings sweeping overhead, but she couldn't make out the bird. She wanted it to be an owl. At camp, she and Barrett took their binoculars at dusk and looked for the owls waking up in the tops of their trees. They had found a mating pair in the spruce trees down by the lake. The male called to the female and then, a minute later, the female called back. They could go for hours like that, the owls, calling back and forth. Tessa and Barrett would sit across from one another, each leaning against a spruce, and make a silent O shape with their mouths, pretending they were the owls.

Tessa thought about turning around. Her pupils felt swollen from the effort of seeing through the softening blackness. The girls still had time to crawl back into their sleeping bags and wake up with the morning reveille, the bells that bristled over the PA system. It was their cabin's turn for sailing, and they were on KP duty, but only at lunch. They had a skit planned for the campfire that night. Tessa and Barrett were playing hummingbirds in a reenactment of a Native American legend. They were going to dive their hands into the air like sharp hummingbird beaks and poke the first stars in the night sky. Tessa reached out to tap Barrett's shoulder, but then she heard the bounce of her friend's backpack, the excitement as Barrett rose up on her toes to take the next step in their journey. Barrett had been planning their trip, she called it, for weeks. As soon as Tessa said alright, Barrett brought out the maps she must've packed from home. She drew dashes in rainbow colors along their route from camp to one little town and then the next. Tessa remembered the maps in Barrett's backpack and let her arm fall back to her side.

When they reached the sign, *Camp Weyamucca—Gem of the California Sierras*, Barrett aimed the flashlight at her hand signal, "okay." She meant they could speak. They stood along a narrow dirt road.

"Are we doing this?" Tessa said.

"We did it," Barrett said, her eyes glossy in the flashlight's shine.

Barrett could turn five cartwheels across a lawn, one after another, and land on her feet with both arms stretched high above her head like Olga Korbut. Tessa could do only two in a row before her head fuzzed and softened as if it could drift away from her.

"Are you nervous?" Tessa said. She pulled her jacket close to her sides. She wore it inside out so the Camp Weyamucca seal didn't show.

"Don't be nervous," Barrett said.

"I don't want to be," Tessa said.

Barrett reached for Tessa's hand, and they walked the few miles to town like schoolgirls.

The counselors would search camp first: the cabins, archery range, campfire area, the docks, and swimming raft. And then the boys' camp across the lake. Last summer, three girls from Cabin Perseverance canoed over to the boys' cabins at midnight. They were discovered the next morning, asleep under blankets in a canoe tied to the boys' dock. The camp director sent the girls home. At morning council, she lectured the rest of them. She wouldn't stand for canoodling. Barrett and Tessa sat on the splintery pine benches amid the rows of girls slumped forward in their *CW* T-shirts. Canoodling in canoes, Barrett whispered, is against the law.

The girls reached the next road, a two-lane strip of asphalt through the middle of the trees. A dull gray dawn turned the pines greenish black, and waking birds chirped from beneath their cover. The service station soon appeared up ahead: an orange-and-blue 76 sign tilted on a white pole. Barrett said someone would need gas and stop. Their plan revolved around this gas station.

The 76 sign reminded Tessa of home.

"We're almost there," she said. She fiddled with the teardrop amethyst pendant on the gold chain around her neck. A present from her parents.

If she called her father, he'd drive the eight hours from Danville, pick them up in the station wagon straightaway, but Barrett had said how they went was as important as leaving. Every few days Tessa's father sent her postcards at camp from the dog. The dog missed her as much as he loved chasing Mrs. Fielsted's orange cat. He made a show of fetching balls and foraging in her mother's petunias as if he didn't. He said the red petunias with yellow stripes tasted like sugar snap peas. Her mother wouldn't let him sleep in Tessa's spot on the couch in the den. Her mother had gone to Weyamucca when she was a girl. She remembered all the songs like it was yesterday. She sent care packages with crumbled molasses cookies and Mad Libs Tessa hadn't played since fourth grade. The same as her mother, Tessa's dead grandmother, had sent when she was a camper.

The gas station had two pumps with rusted handles. Scratched-up glass covered the black numbers that rolled up to nine and then back to zero when the gas was flowing. A vending machine leaned against a mechanics garage attached to a small office. Two panes were cracked in the office window, and Tessa considered whether the place had been abandoned. Town wasn't a town, it was the gas station and the post office outlet and a bait-and-tackle shack farther up the road. The camp van had stopped at the shack last summer on the way back from a hike up Mount Shasta. The counselors wanted to use the pay phone. They sent the girls inside for Popsicles from the freezer in the back of the bait shop. Half the freezer was stocked with Drumsticks and Bomb Pops and the other with frozen trout, the crystal fish eyes staring as the girls reached in for their treat.

Barrett slotted two quarters through the vending machine and pushed the button for a Coke.

"We'll split," she said.

Tessa wasn't thirsty.

"When do they open?" Tessa said, looking at the dirt and gravel driveways around the pumps and leading into the garage.

"Eight," Barrett said. Though like Tessa, she only knew about the gas station from what she could see. A puddle filled a divot in the gravel between the pumps and the building. The smoky, sharp petroleum scent bloomed around them. Tessa's Timex with the Velcro band showed six o'clock.

"You think it'll take till then to get our ride?" Tessa said. She reached for the Coke, drank two big sips. Tessa forgot phone numbers and directions; she scribbled reminders on the back of her hand. Barrett didn't forget, but she liked to decorate their calves with anklets in ballpoint. Sometimes they drew lines of flowers along each other's arms or a secret symbol of the boys they liked above one knee. Glasses for Tessa's crush, and a baseball for Barrett's. Last night as a joke, Barrett had written the address of where they were going—the purple star on the map—in permanent marker above Tessa's right hipbone, where no one could see it.

Barrett shrugged, and both girls looked up and then down the road.

Headlights approached as if summoned from the direction of Camp Weyamucca. A small gray Toyota pickup turned into the gas station and parked alongside the garage. The bottom half of the truck was spattered with mud. A boy got out. He had a crew cut and wore a button-down short-sleeved shirt with a 76 on one side and on the other an oval patch that read *Tom*. Barrett and Tessa had stepped behind the vending machine, but he was close enough to read.

The boy straightened the collar of his shirt as if he'd just put it on, tucked a pack of cigarettes in the right sleeve, and then walked around the vending machine to where the girls waited by the garage. He was only a few years older. His pants were worn in the knees and streaked with dried mud, as were the boots he wore with laces loose and frayed. Acne clustered on his cheeks, and his orange hair looked stiff as straw. He blinked at them slowly, like a toad. His eyes were blue and he had thick pale eyelids.

"You girls are from the camp, aren't you?" he said.

Barrett and Tessa looked at each other.

"You must be confusing us with someone else," Tessa said. She talked to the dim, unattractive boys and Barrett the clever, good-looking ones. Barrett had cheekbones and blond hair and early puberty.

"I've worked there, washing dishes in the kitchen," he said.

Tessa nodded like her mother would. Barrett watched the empty road beyond the boy.

"What are you, runaways?" he said.

"What do you want to know about us for?" Barrett said. She sipped the Coke and then wiped her upper lip with the back of her hand.

Barrett's lips curved into a heart, but the boy didn't look at her any differently than he looked at Tessa.

"I open up the station in the morning and there's you all here, and it's my responsibility to know which way this is going," he said. His eyelids opened and closed slow again, saying he didn't care which way it went.

"You don't have reason to think about us," Tessa said. "We'll be gone the first car that comes and takes us."

Barrett elbowed Tessa in the ribs hard enough that Tessa cringed. She turned and caught the gold flints in Barrett's green eyes.

"It's alright, I'm not a talker," the boy said, and smiled. He had a split between his two front teeth. "Fact is, though, no one's gonna want you."

"We've got money," Barrett said.

"That's good," the boy said. "But you're pretty girls. Could be kidnapping. People traveling around here don't want trouble. They come to get rid of it."

"We just need a ride to meet our parents in Red Bluff," Tessa said.

"How'd you get up here when your parents are down there?" he said. He crossed his arms in front and stood wide like he was daring them.

"Our parents' friends were driving us, but their car broke," Tessa said.

The boy tilted his head to look at the evergreen branches scratching against the gas station. The wind had come up and the trees swayed.

"Might work," he said.

"When do people start coming in for gas?" Barrett said.

The boy shrugged. He looked up and down the road. Yellow morning light swept over the top of the forest.

"I've been meaning to get down to Red Bluff. My mother's birthday is coming, and I want to get her something nice," he said.

❋   ❋   ❋

They sat three across in the truck, Tessa in the middle. The drive from Red Bluff to camp took five hours on the camp bus from the Safeway parking lot where parents dropped off their girls and hugged them goodbye for the month. This morning they were headed south on 85, down from the mountains, and Tom drove fast. He said it would take them four hours, tops. Tessa leaned toward Barrett, but on the curves she couldn't help her leg pushing against Tom's. His thigh felt like one strong muscle. When Tessa and Barrett were alone the few minutes it took Tom to unlock the office and call in sick to his boss, they agreed their plan had worked. "I told you we'd find a ride," Barrett said, but she wasn't preening. By the time he dropped them off and drove back to Weyamucca, if he worked there, they'd be far south. On their way to Hollywood.

They were going to Sunset and Doheny, where Barrett's cousin lived. Barrett's cousin wore knee-high boots with miniskirts and worked on costumes for movies. Barrett visited once and took a picture of her cousin's closet stuffed with silk pantsuits, little sequin dresses, and platform shoes. She swore she was going back as soon as her parents let her, but it had been over a year and her parents said they didn't see the point of Los Angeles. All those freeways and palm trees growing out of dirt squares in the cement. But Barrett didn't care what they thought. She and Tessa would lie on her bed, staring at the photograph of her cousin's closet and imagine zipping their legs into shiny white boots.

Tom lit one of his cigarettes, the end burning orange and black. Tessa inhaled the smoke and let the wind from the open windows whip her hair around as they rushed downhill. She forgot the Camp Weyamucca sailboats and her father's station wagon in the heat coming off Tom's leg and the sparkling wardrobe in Barrett's cousin's closet. She felt like she could be in the movies. It was hard to remember that a few hours ago she had wanted to climb back into her sleeping bag. Tom held out his cigarette to Tessa, and if she thought she could inhale without choking, she'd have taken it. She shook her head. He didn't offer any to Barrett, who was looking out her window into the canyons of skeletal pine trees, their green majesty eaten out by tiny beetles. She seemed sealed up in her world as if they were already on the bus with strangers. She might be thinking about Los Angeles, or the next dotted line on her maps, or a thing Tessa couldn't guess. Tessa liked sitting between Barrett and Tom as if she was the one responsible, the connection, for getting this ride.

They reached the foothills, rolling mounds of scrub brush and short, scraggly pines. The highway ran straight toward a vacant horizon as if Red Bluff didn't exist yet. The morning was established now, hot, dry air pouring in through the windows. Tessa wished they'd bought another Coke from the vending machine.

She felt Tom's right foot press down on the gas as he pulled out to pass an RV. Its bumper sticker read, *NO SHIRT, NO SHOES*. Tom laughed.

"That's the life."

The truck swayed left, then right, as he slid around the RV and back into the lane. Tessa reached out for the dashboard so she wouldn't fall into his lap. There was a rectangular hole with red and black wires sticking out instead of a radio.

"What happened to the radio?" she said. She'd been waiting to ask.

Barrett looked out her window.

"I bought the truck from a guy, radio never worked. I was driving one day and the fuzz was going on it and I threw it out the window. Tore the wires with my teeth."

Tessa felt Barrett's sigh. The teeth were a child's bragging, or he was joking and hadn't got the rhythm. When they were still in the mountains, Barrett had nudged two bottles rolling around the footwell against Tessa's feet. An empty liquor bottle and a full one. The liquor was amber-colored and thin as water.

"Why don't you get a new radio?" Barrett said. Tessa was the only one who knew she wanted to be a singer.

"I haven't found the one I want."

Tom opened his palm on the steering wheel. Freckles covered the backs of his hands and ran into the arm of his jacket and then crawled out his collar. If Tessa looked at him from the side, the acne blended with the freckles as if it wasn't there. She had eleven freckles on her nose. The doctor told her mother she'd grow out of them.

"Besides, I like the quiet," Tom said. "I hear my thoughts."

"I know what you mean," Tessa said. Barrett elbowed her side, and this time Tessa nudged her back. She knew what he meant. She didn't tell Barrett everything that came to her mind. She wondered if Barrett had noticed Tom offer her a cigarette.

"I like music, don't get me wrong. But when I'm driving—" He took a last drag on the cigarette burned down to a stub and threw it out the window. "That bumper sticker on the RV, for example, got me thinking," Tom said.

"About what?" Tessa said. Barrett leaned her head against the passenger window and closed her eyes.

"Usually it's posted on a sign, like in a restaurant: 'No Shirt, No Shoes, No Service,'" he said. "Here, they left off the 'service.' They don't want any. They don't care about pleasing. But everybody stands up to the boss, so what?"

He paused and Tessa wondered if she was supposed to answer, but then he went on.

"The part that gets me is the words themselves."

"No shirt, no shoes," Tessa said carefully, as if to learn from it.

"They're *free birds*. You get it?" He looked over, his blue eyes lit up. She wondered what his mouth tasted like. She'd never kissed someone with red hair and that many freckles.

"They're doing whatever they want," she said.

"And wearing what they want. Or maybe nothing. They could be nudists. Driving from one colony to the next, stripped down naked."

Tessa felt her cheeks flare with color. Naked people in an RV. She laughed.

"Is that what they are?"

"I don't know, but I like to think they might be," he said. He turned to her again and smiled. The gap in his teeth made his face interesting, his own kind of handsome. "Maybe we should go back and ask them?"

"No!" she said. She covered her mouth with her hands as if shocked or embarrassed, though she wasn't.

"I bet they'd take us to some parties," he said. He checked the mirrors and flicked on his blinker like he was going to turn around.

Tessa touched his shoulder, her fingers on the crease above his bicep.

"No, no! Please!" she said.

He shrugged and grinned and shifted in his seat, clicked off the blinker. "If you say so. But that could've been a good time we missed out on."

They fell back into quiet. Tessa wished for the missing radio, sound to reunite them. She felt Barrett's body beside her, heavy with sleep. She could sleep anywhere.

Tom checked his watch and looked up at the sky as if he'd heard words from it, or a new thought had come down from there and gathered his attention.

Tessa considered the sky, cloudless and still, and where his mind had drifted. When he spoke again she felt hopeful, until she realized his words.

"Why don't you reach down there and see what we've got?" he said, and pointed to the whiskey bottle wedged behind Barrett's Tretorns.

※　　※　　※

They drove from the foothills into flat, endless acres of dull grasses and sagebrush. Power lines ran alongside the highway, dipping from tower to tower. Tessa sat up straight in the seat and watched each tower grow taller as they sped toward it and then disappear as the truck shot past. Tom steered with one hand at the bottom of the wheel, with the other he balanced the whiskey bottle on his leg, as if this position was common and reliable. For Tessa, it was her first time trying whiskey, or liquor of any kind.

The brown liquid fired down her throat, even when she allowed only a trickle in her mouth. Tom didn't encourage her to drink, but he handed her the bottle and that was enough. He kept the bottle longer on his turns, pointed its neck in the direction of rivers he liked to fish and the lonely tire tracks that led to them. Tessa couldn't make out any distant gullies in the scorched land or pockets of cottonwood trees or other signs of water. Though she imagined him alone on a riverbank at sunset—his favorite time, he said, to fish—casting a rod into a pocket of gurgling river, and then the line catching and him arching back, muscles rippled beneath his shirt as he reeled in a silver trout.

Tessa felt the alcohol zing in her head. She turned older with each sip, her body smooth, pliant, ready. If the radio worked, she would turn it loud. Or not. She didn't want Barrett to wake up. Barrett's golden hair had fallen over half her face. She couldn't feel it tickling her cheek, or hear them talking.

"She's a real sleeper," Tom said.

"The car knocks her out. She sleeps the whole way to camp and the whole way back." She caught the word, *camp*. "I mean the campsite where we go with our parents."

"That's okay," he said.

"That's okay, what?" She spoke softly. She didn't want to sound like a drunken kid. Tom handed her the bottle again and their fingers touched as she took it. His skin was rough. He had working hands. She drank this time for real and barely felt the burn.

"I don't care about your business," he said.

"We're going to Red Bluff to get a bus to Los Angeles. Barrett has a cousin who works in the movies."

"You want to be in the movies?"

She shrugged. Maybe she did. He asked as if her being an actress was a possibility.

"Barrett likes it there, and I've never been and camp was a drag." She handed him the whiskey, the side of her up against him though the highway ran straight as an arrow across the withered fields. When she let go of the bottle, she let her arm brush his leg. She felt they were inches, minutes, from their first kiss. If he didn't have to keep his eyes on the road, if Barrett wasn't on the other side of her.

"I woke up this morning like it was any other day," he said. "And then I meet a girl like you."

❋   ❋   ❋

They drank half the bottle. Or Tom did, with her help. Then he screwed the cap on tight with one hand, his other balancing the wheel. He didn't want them to get shitfaced, he said.

Tessa giggled. She couldn't help it. He told her to put the bottle back

SMALL IN REAL LIFE

careful, so she didn't wake Sleeping Beauty. She slid the bottle beneath Barrett's legs as quiet as a mouse. Tom handed her a stick of gum. He asked her questions: what she liked to do (lie on her bed and listen to records), her favorite color (turquoise), the food she could eat every day and never get tired of. She said milkshakes, which didn't make sense, as she'd get sick of milkshakes, but it was hot in the truck and that's what came into her head, liquid thick with cold. He told her about his father leaving when he was ten and his mother working jobs till late at night. Tessa didn't know anyone who'd lost a parent. He said it wasn't like that, his father wasn't dead, just gone. There was a difference.

Barrett woke up as they turned off the freeway and slowed for traffic. She yawned and stretched and stared out at the Red Bluff car dealerships. Tessa and Tom were looking ahead out the window, enjoying the easy silence between them, Tessa thought. She felt like Barrett had slept through months, too long to catch up. She chewed the spearmint gum Tom had given her and waited long enough for Barrett's eyes to adjust to the light shining off the rows of windshields in the parking lots.

"Tom will drop us off at the bus station," Tessa said.

Tom had both freckled hands around the wheel, at ten and two as Tessa's father had taught her.

"It's not far. I've got a stop to make on the way," he said.

Barrett smoothed her hair back into a ponytail and looped a pink elastic band from her wrist around it.

"Where?" she said.

"Tom's picking up that present for his mom," Tessa said. Her tongue was thick with the whiskey. She tried to separate her words.

"Her birthday's the day after tomorrow," Tom said. It was as if they were making up a story. But Tom had a mother, and it was her birthday.

Barrett looked at her and Tessa looked back. She studied the black dots in the center of Barrett's glowing eyes. She twisted her mouth to say, Like we have another option. Barrett sighed and turned to her window.

"I'm hungry," Tessa said. She was starving. After the drive with Tom in the truck, she sensed she would feel only in extremes. She'd be starving, exhausted, desperate. And she could see things differently. Red Bluff, for example, was uglier than she remembered. Low, flat buildings with pipes sticking out the top of them. The dust from the dry, brittle land underneath seeping up over the cement into the desert air. The midday sun glazed the storefronts yellow. In the next block, they passed the Safeway parking lot. Cars turned in and out of the driveway; people walked toward the market to buy their gallon of milk. Tessa didn't want to linger here looking for a bus or a ride. What if Tom drove them straight through to LA?

"Get out a sandwich," Barrett said. They'd packed cheese sandwiches from yesterday's lunch.

"Don't feel like it," Tessa said. She wanted a hamburger.

"We'll get food at the station," Barrett said. She pulled her backpack onto her lap, opened and closed pockets confirming their contents.

"You have enough money?" Tom said.

"We have enough," Barrett said.

Tessa had given Barrett the twenty-three dollars she had left of the cash her mother packed her for the camp store. She didn't know how much they had altogether. Or the cost of bus fare to Hollywood. Once she agreed to go, she had trusted Barrett. It was her idea, her cousin, her maps that would get them through.

"To go all the way to Los Angeles?" Tom said.

"Who said we were going there?" Barrett said. But she didn't elbow Tessa. She held the backpack and looked ahead out the window.

Tom ducked and peered at the stores as if he were checking addresses or hoping for a certain place to identify itself.

"I heard it around," he said.

"He guessed," Tessa said, like she had no part in it. "He won't tell." Hunger drew her stomach into an ache. Her leg rested against Tom's as if it had come that way, heavy and unmovable and dependent. On her other side, Barrett had shifted toward the door. There were inches of vinyl seat between them.

"I mind myself," Tom said.

Barrett had her hand on the door handle, her other hand on her backpack.

"Let us out."

"Barrett, it's fine. Relax," Tessa said, her tongue rolling over in her mouth.

"Let us out, now," Barrett said.

Tom drove on as if she'd said nothing.

"Barrett, calm down. We're going to stop at this store and then we'll go to the bus," Tessa said.

Barrett looked at her, studied her eyes, but Tessa knew they wouldn't give way. Her eyes were wide open. She could see the line indented on Barrett's cheek from sleeping against the side of the truck.

"We don't have time," Barrett said.

"We have all the time," Tessa said. It was her trip as much as Barrett's.

"That doesn't make sense—you're not making sense."

"Because I'm not doing what you want?"

"What are you talking about?"

Tom slowed at the curb, in front of a jewelry store.

"Here we are," he said. He leaned forward and looked at them. Tessa watched his eyes slide from Barrett's face down her long neck and over her chest before he turned to Tessa.

"You're gonna help me pick something out, right?" he said. And then to Barrett, "She's got that pretty necklace. I could use her advice."

Tessa touched the amethyst on her chain, felt for the tiny diamonds around her birthstone.

Barrett sat up in her seat and tightened her ponytail.

"There's always a woman in these stores, and she'll have advice for you," Barrett said. "We've got to get to the station."

Tom reached over Tessa and opened the glove box in front of Barrett. He smelled like cigarettes and gasoline and whiskey. He pulled out a baseball cap, knocked the glove box shut, and slid the hat on his head.

"It'll only take a minute," he said.

"We've got to go," Barrett said, her lips pursed. Tessa could barely see the heart in them.

"Only a minute," Tessa said, bargaining with her endless time. She wanted to look at necklaces with Tom. More than she wanted to go to Los Angeles, more than she wanted anything.

"Then I'll take you girls to catch your bus to Hollywood," Tom said.

"I don't think it's a good idea," Barrett said quietly, just for Tessa.

"I don't mind," Tessa said.

She smiled at Barrett as if she were helping the three of them out, doing this one favor.

Tom got out and Tessa slid across his seat into the street. She followed him around the front of the truck and held up her finger to show Barrett she'd take a minute and not any more. Barrett stared from behind the windshield and shook her head.

The store was air-conditioned. A glass counter ran along each side and another across the back. An older woman stood at the back counter, polishing a watch. Permed ash-blond ringlets clung around her pale face. Her cheeks were shiny, or oily, like she'd put on Vaseline instead of makeup. Over her eyes, she'd penciled brown eyebrows with sharp peaks.

"Good morning, ma'am," Tom said.

The woman smiled. "Good morning," she said, and the eyebrows climbed her forehead. On her wrist she wore a yellow plastic coil bunched with small keys.

"I brought my girlfriend to help find a necklace for my momma's birthday," Tom said. He put his arm around Tessa, drew her shoulder snug under his armpit. A lightness burst down her arms and legs, into her toes. She'd never been held and owned.

"She's lovely." The woman's brown eyes were moist and receding. Her arm quivered, a mild tremble, and the keys around her wrist bounced faintly on the glass counter.

When Tom spoke again, his voice boomed above the whir of the air conditioner mounted in the window behind the woman.

"We'd like to look at your gold necklaces," Tom said.

The woman picked through her keys and then slid them into locks and opened the sliding panels on two of the cases. She reached in for the necklaces dangling on velvet stands. She pulled one out and then another and another, arranged them on top of the glass.

Tom leaned forward to examine the gold chains. Some had round links and others S shapes that fit right together as if they'd been glued. Each chain had a pendant. There were open gold hearts, circles of diamonds, and blue sapphire stars. Tessa didn't see any amethysts.

"Momma loves diamonds," Tom said.

"I've never met a woman who doesn't," the woman said. "My favorite are the initials. Pave, they call it. It's the style of setting those little diamonds close together."

"Do you have a 'D' for 'Doreen'?" Tom said. A gold chain with a diamond D hung from the third necklace stand on the counter. Tom could see it as well as Tessa.

He watched the woman peer down into the cases and then pause above the one case she hadn't opened yet. It held what Tessa's mom would call fine jewelry: engagement rings, bracelets, earrings, and necklaces glittering with diamonds under the store lights. The diamonds were large and white. When the woman moved past the expensive jewelry and back toward Tessa and Tom, Tessa heard Tom's breath going in hard and then coming out fast like he was angry. The woman examined the displays she'd already set in front of them and found the D.

"Here it is," she said. Tom smiled as if he were grateful and took the necklace. He held it out in front of Tessa like you would a sweater to see if it was the right size.

"It's nice," Tessa said, as his girlfriend in the jewelry store.

"You didn't need her help after all," the woman said.

"Moral support," Tom said, and drew Tessa to him again so they admired the necklace dangling from his hand together. She caught the tang of his odor and felt dampness under his arm.

He set the D necklace back on its stand and pointed at another, in the case with all the diamonds.

"I'd like to see my girl wearing that one," he said. "Can we try it?"

The three of them looked down through the glass. Tom had chosen a necklace made only of diamonds, one after the other building in size from either side until they met in the middle around one giant sparkling jewel, as if designed for a princess.

"He's going to spoil you," the woman said. She unlocked the glass case and set the necklace on the counter.

Tom lifted the diamonds from the velvet and opened the clasp. He moved behind Tessa and rested the cold stones on her skin. She gathered her hair and held it up for him. His fingers glanced the back of her neck and she shivered. When he finished, the woman crossed her hands over her heart.

"Dear, look in the mirror," the woman said to Tessa. "It's breathtaking."

Tessa turned to the framed mirror on the counter. She looked like she was playing dress-up with her mother's jewelry box. That is if her mother had owned fancy jewelry. But when she looked up from the necklace to her straight lips and her freckled nose and her almond eyes, she could no longer see the librarian. She hesitated on her features, where they had altered, then Tom spoke.

"We'd better get going," he said.

"I can wrap your gift up nice," the woman said. She picked up the necklace for Tom's mother and hurried through the door in the back of the store.

Tom reached in his back pocket and shook out a crumpled plastic bag.

"You be quiet now," he said to Tessa.

He walked behind the glass counters and tried the sliding doors. He smiled when they opened. The woman had left them unlocked, every one, as he'd intended. He started with the diamonds, reached in and grabbed at the rings and watches and bracelets and necklaces. Then he shook out the velvet displays left on the counter. The necklaces dropped into the bag like worthless candy.

Tessa watched Tom. He rushed to the next cases as the air turned thick and balled up around her like cotton.

"She's slow as shit, but she'll be back and we'd better be gone. You wanna help me?"

The air conditioner shuddered to a stop. Tessa didn't know if he'd asked her a question. If he expected her to bend down beside him and reach under the display lights and swipe at the hoop earrings and little ring stands. She'd never work as fast with him as he could alone. Tom cleared the last case and turned at the door, his plastic bag swinging from one fist. He glared as if she were a child who had disobeyed. She was meant to follow him.

"You're not good for much," he said. He grabbed her arm and led her out the door into the white daylight. She winced at the brightness. She felt him guide her into the street, around the truck. She heard the door open, and then he shoved her inside and climbed in after her. He started the truck, and they jerked away from the curb, into the passing traffic.

When Tessa's eyes opened, she realized that she had not thought about Barrett once, and then, that Barrett wasn't in the truck.

"Looks like she abandoned you," Tom said. He yanked the buttons off his shirt with the "Tom" on it, shrugged it from his shoulders, and dropped the shirt out his open window. He had a gray T-shirt on underneath. She'd never noticed.

"My name's Mark," he said.

Barrett and Tessa had decided that if they were split up, they would meet at the apartment. She had the address in black ink above her hip. *1125 Doheny Drive.*

Tessa slid over to Barrett's side of the truck. She didn't know about the real Tom, if he was tied up in a ditch or searching his dresser for his missing 76 shirt and keys. Or if Mark was Tom turning over another leaf. She wouldn't need an alias for robbing the jewelry store. Had she robbed it? The necklace sat heavy on her chest. The woman in the store didn't know her name, of course, just what she looked like.

"You can't count on girls like that," he said. "They can't help it. They've had too many advantages."

Tessa imagined Barrett leaving the truck and walking alone down the sidewalk, away from the jewelry store. When she tried to see Barrett's face, what she was thinking, Barrett wasn't Barrett anymore. It worked better if Tessa watched a stranger come and take Barrett from the truck, and she was slapping and kicking him but he was big and strong and no one came to stop him. Tessa wouldn't know unless she got to Hollywood and found out whether Barrett was there, or not. But she didn't have any money, only a princess's necklace.

He kept checking the rearview mirror and out the side windows.

"I'm sorry about what I said in the store. You played your part better than if I'd told you what to do," he said. "I get hot in the head when it's time to go, don't mean anything by it. Adrenaline."

His eyes ran over her as they had on Barrett, her face, her neck, her chest.

"You look pretty in that necklace," he said.

Tessa's hand went to the necklace, its hard, cut stones. In the windshield she could see the diamonds reflected, flinty in the sunlight.

"Take it off now," he said.

She reached behind her neck and tried for the clasp. There were two parts, a latch to unhook and then a button to push that released the necklace. Her fingernails were too short to lift the latch but she kept trying, while he rapped a thumb against the steering wheel.

"That's alright," he said. "Let's try this." He lifted the neck of her T-shirt, his fingers soft on her collarbone, and tucked the shirt up and around the diamonds.

The covered necklace pressed into her.

"You want to eat? We'll drive a little ways. There's a place that has the best milkshakes I ever tasted. My daddy used to take me there, before he left, when I was a kid. I didn't ask which flavor you like, vanilla or chocolate?" Tom said.

Tessa searched the sidewalks for Barrett with her backpack slung over her shoulders. The up and down glide of her steps, her backpack floating behind her. Tessa slipped her fingers inside the waist of her jeans, but she couldn't feel Barrett's handwriting on her skin. She wondered if later a stranger would find the address on her body and believe it could solve a crime.

The boy was watching her, his blue eyes fierce on her.

"What flavor you like?" he said.

The sun bore down on the stucco buildings, on the squinting cars ahead. The glare reached into the truck and spread over Tessa until she breathed the stale heat and it coated her lungs with invisible dust. She looked out the window for the bus station or Barrett or a police car or a sign to follow back to where she had started that morning, alone in the trees with her best friend, walking through the dark.

GOD'S WORK

✳   ✳   ✳

Rebecca Hansen certainly was not this woman's name. A Rebecca Hansen organized fundraisers for children with cancer and carried a pocketbook that snapped shut decisively when she was finished with it. Morrison decided this woman was an Elaine, scented feminine like potpourri. She finished each sentence with a nervous giggle, and her unease made Morrison feel old and tired. She watched him carefully, examining what, he couldn't imagine. He drank his two glasses of pinot before they finished their salads. The restaurant tables around them were full of people, but he didn't recognize anyone. It was only Tuesday. He raised his empty wineglass and nodded at the waiter standing in the corner. He would take a cab home.

The waiter cleared their salad plates, and Rebecca ordered another cosmopolitan. As if she were twenty-two instead of sixtysomething trying to pass as a free-spirited midfifties. An artist living in a bungalow in Pasadena, he thought, but she wasn't. She wore a low-cut sweater the color of peach sherbet. It showed off her sunspotted chest, and he didn't look further. Her bright gold hair was pinned back on each side with barrettes, and orange feather and bead earrings dangled from her ears. Morrison drew his eyes back to her round face and watched a clump of blue mascara stuck on her right eyelash.

She leaned across the table toward Morrison and paused like she might confess a secret. Flirting. He tried to discern her intentions: some imagined happily ever after or simply a free dinner. Either way, he didn't trust her. She may have possessed wisdom beneath her years, but so did he.

"Tell me," she said, and giggled. "What does a judge do?"

Morrison had never known a Barnard girl, woman, to wear blue mascara. It crossed his mind that Rebecca had anticipated this unlikelihood and worn the mascara anyway. He took a sip of water and let the cold run down his throat. She watched him with those brown eyes, the outer corners drooped like a basset hound's. She was not afraid to look at him dead on, which was more than he could say for some women. He decided to treat her like a plaintiff; he owed her courtesy.

"I read papers the lawyers write," he said. "I listen to them make their case in court. I try to get the important details laid out so I or the jury can make an informed decision according to the laws." He could say these words in his sleep. Everyone wanted to know. What about the robe? It's hot in the summer, he answered, and I'm not saying whether I've gone naked underneath. He was willowy and blue-eyed, and his wife's friends had blushed when he told them. But the administration of justice was not provocative. Civil court crept along, hindering progress every day. As its officer, he delivered a diminished reckoning. Many days he looked out from his second-floor office at the patch of grass bordering the cement sidewalk across the street—our green space, his secretary Geraldine called it—and wondered what he had done to deserve such tedium. Then he tried to believe that things had worked out for him as well as he had any right to expect.

"Have you ever sentenced someone to death?" Rebecca played with one of the feather earrings, twisted the beads back and forth between two fingers.

"There hasn't been an execution in California for years. It's life imprisonment." In his dating profile, Geraldine had simply typed *JUDGE* for occupation. His civil court decisions had bankrupted a few men; an attorney once called his verdict a death sentence.

"Murderers get life in prison," Rebecca said. She let go of the earring to pick up her drink. She'd ordered her next round before finishing the first. He considered that they both were attempting to improve their respective evenings. The pink-red of the cosmopolitan clashed with her peach lipstick, though the lipstick matched the sweater. Morrison didn't understand the orange feather earrings.

"I would say yes. These are people who committed terrible crimes."

Rebecca's watery brown eyes focused on his face.

"What's the worst crime you've seen in court?"

Morrison looked for the waiter, for his wine, but the man had retreated to the kitchen.

"Well, murder for one." A bald-faced lie, Geraldine would say, but what did he have to lose. "I will spare you the details, but the man was convicted."

"An eye for an eye," she said, and if she hadn't nodded, he might have considered her dismissive.

"You can be assured, he went to prison."

"He was very guilty," Rebecca said, and fiddled with her earring again, massaged the beads gently as if rubbing a magic lantern. For a moment, he considered the remote look on her face and what she wished for, but to his relief, his curiosity passed.

"I don't know that there's a *very* or *not so much* with murder. The question comes down to what the accused did or didn't do." And at this, Rebecca blanched. She released the earring and took a drink of the cosmopolitan. When she set the drink down, her eyes searched for some object behind him. Perhaps she missed the waiter, too.

"But there can be extenuating circumstances," she said. "Or insanity."

Insanity. She wouldn't let a ponderous subject rest. Why had he come? He was concerned about his good name: he was a public figure after all, of sorts. He had yelled at Geraldine, and he was not a yeller, when she first showed him the website. She'd used a photo from last year's California Bar conference. He looked tidy and dull in a gray suit and striped tie. At the conference, he had spoken on a panel about judicial discretion in jurisdictional disputes. Boring as hell, he'd thought then, and still did. The waiter finally appeared from the kitchen, and Morrison caught the man's eye. The waiter nodded and hurried to the bar. Morrison only counted glasses for Geraldine, and she wasn't sitting here at dinner with Rebecca Hansen. He sensed that certain colleagues had expected his drinking might ease after his son's accident. But one more glass of wine had never made a particular difference either way for Morrison, or his judgment.

"I suppose any circumstance can be extenuating."

Rebecca straightened in her chair and folded a piece of gold hair behind her ear. She was composing herself as if something had come loose between them; he couldn't sense what. He had been distracted by his thoughts.

"On TV shows they get to explain what happened," she said, as if television was a matter of fact.

The waiter arrived with their drinks, a plate of spaghetti bolognese, and Morrison's branzino. The fish was pan-seared with olive oil and seasoned with lemon and salt.

"Everyone has a right to an attorney, but there are laws. It's not show-and-tell like *Perry Mason*." He ate the branzino attentively, a few white flakes at a time.

Rebecca's brows furrowed. He had confused her.

❋   ❋   ❋

Morrison had felt Geraldine hovering in the doorway of his office that afternoon. She only waited for him to acknowledge her if she had done something wrong. He did not look up.

"Judge?"

Morrison scanned a Motion to Dismiss. "Yes?"

Geraldine's gabardine skirt swished against its liner as she entered his office. The Chamber, they called it, a cavernous room with massive dark furniture. It would take a crane to move his desk alone. The furniture had been there fifty years, inherited with the job. At the law firm he had dictated appellate briefs from a corner office on the thirty-fourth floor, paced before windows that stretched to the ceiling as junior partners and senior associates scribbled his words—astute and decisive—on yellow pads. But he preferred to remember that period, its liveliness and authority, as a stepping-stone to the calm, numbing regularity of the Los Angeles Superior Court. He was a respected public servant: the Honorable Charles Morrison.

SMALL IN REAL LIFE

Geraldine set a coffee mug on his desk. She kept him at a cup a day, and he'd had coffee that morning. His eyes slid over the milky brown; he knew she'd added the Sweet'N Low forbidden most days, a distant association she'd made to cancer. For a moment, he wondered if she'd issued bail to a wayward stranger in need from church without asking him. But Geraldine believed that people should pay for their sins. She would not borrow the weight of his office for her own version of God's work. Morrison reached for the coffee and waited for her to tell him she'd double-booked his court calendar. The woman kept his aging heart beating, but she could not prevent the weeks of March from colliding.

He sipped the coffee and looked at her over the black rims of his bifocals.

"Judge, I have done right by you today."

"You do right by me every day."

Her pale brown eyes watched him as she straightened the papers in his outbox. "I have made a reservation for two at Giuseppe's."

"Ah, your man is playing poker. If you let me have a glass of pinot—make it two glasses—you may tell me about the latest lost soul you've converted to St. John the Baptist."

Geraldine smiled, waved a hand in the air. "No redeemed children of God for you tonight." Then she crossed her arms, rocked forward in her sensible shoes, and said, "Miss Rebecca Hansen will be joining you."

"I don't know any Miss Rebecca—" And in saying the name, he knew. "Oh, Geraldine."

Geraldine shook her head; she never conceded to an error in judgment. Not that she should. He often thought she was the more worthy arbiter of justice. Never a doubt in her mind. God-gives-me-strength-and-wisdom-and-love-and-there-isn't-any-more-to-be-had-in-this-world. Geraldine spoke to him now: "Miss Rebecca is a lovely woman of fifty-five years who enjoys the symphony and does not prefer the opera."

"I told you to take that foolishness off the internet."

"Sir, Miss Rebecca sent you a note. She wanted to meet. She liked your honesty. She appreciated your good taste. Now listen to me, Judge, this is a good-looking single woman of the appropriate age who went to Barnard. She is smart!"

"No, Geraldine."

"She was the only response, her message came in seconds before you would have disappeared forever."

"Cancel the dinner."

Geraldine stood above Morrison but she did not look down on him. He felt her look through, into his faded heart.

"With all due respect, and you know I respect you more than any other old man I know, I will not. The reservation is for seven-thirty."

He heard her collect her purse, then the rhythmic squeak of the sneakers she wore to and from work receded to the elevators down the hall and disappeared into silence. She left him to his fate. Morrison worked until seven and drove to the restaurant. The maître d' showed him to a table in the corner, where he found a nervous woman sitting in the candlelight. Rebecca looked at him with such relief that he wished only to return to his desk and make the decision to cancel instead. She reminded him of a TV game show contestant you knew was going to lose in the first round.

He cursed Geraldine as he gently shook Rebecca's outstretched hand. Her fingers were cold and slippery.

"For a minute there, I worried you might not show up," she said, and tittered.

*   *   *

Morrison's wife had gone to Barnard—Geraldine had the idea to list the school as one of his "Likes" on the dating site—and she hadn't worn much makeup. Lipstick. But after his wife died, Morrison visited bars on Ventura Boulevard, places Geraldine didn't know about, and he had seen blue mascara. The women he met in Van Nuys bars lived in apartments with musty wall-to-wall carpeting and worked as beauticians. They were divorced from truck drivers and drywall installers. He bought them piña coladas with slices of canned pineapple, and they told him they "did hair" or "did makeup." Most of them had tried to be actresses. He'd seen startling headshots in 8x10 picture frames on their nightstands; beautiful women with sparkling eyes, breathy smiles, and full, glossy lips. They haunted the bedroom with youth.

He told the women in Van Nuys he was a corporate lawyer in one of the high-rises downtown. The Wells Fargo building with the red bricks and the slanted roof? They nodded even though they didn't know. He liked them for their pretending: their black eyeliner, patchouli scent, and strappy high-heeled sandals. But he never chose fidgety women like Rebecca.

Rebecca twirled a forkful of spaghetti bolognese against her soupspoon. The left side of her mouth sagged, a lost nerve or worn muscle, and Morrison thought of the clown faces he had seen at the circus when he was a boy. The clowns with the fat red downturned lips. He wondered if they were sad men before they were sad clowns.

"Guilty people sometimes go free," she said, and spun noodles around her fork. It appeared they would have only this one conversation, about sins and retribution. As if the two were clear-cut, known, and occasionally overlooked, rather than complex and layered and unresolved.

"It happens." Morrison didn't want to get caught up in dessert. He looked at his watch.

"I'm afraid I've got work to finish tonight." He smiled, hoping he seemed reluctant yet committed to his duties.

Rebecca's lip twitched. She looked down at her pasta as if he had punished her. The gray hairs sprouting among her dark roots glinted in the candlelight.

But when she looked up at him, her eyes were brighter. One hand casually touched the V-neck dip of her peach sweater. Her intention for the evening crossed his mind again; plaintiffs sought recognition from the court of their rights to something. Her face softened as if to invite an understanding on his part, but he could not read her expression.

"That's too bad. I'm having a nice time." She raised her glass to show him it was empty and bit her lower lip like a teenager. He found himself surprised by her straight white teeth. He was, improbably, stirred.

Because Morrison had gray hair and he didn't blame a woman for aging. It wasn't Rebecca's fault he was sitting with her at the corner table in Giuseppe's. And if he were honest, he wasn't any more bored with her than he would be at home watching the Lakers game with a beer and lasagna heated from the freezer. The facts were such that—he looked at facts, discerning black from white was his job—this woman had been delivered to him for the evening. She wasn't overweight or harsh or difficult. The mystery of her twitching lip was not unintriguing or repellent. He didn't mind the sound of her voice, and her giggling had subsided. When he considered her from this larger picture, he wasn't sorry for her;

he could even overlook her weakness. In reconsidering the facts, he reached the point of equilibrium he sought in adjudicating his cases. The branzino was delicious, and now that he had decided to pay attention, he could see that Rebecca looked at him with admiration that was not cloying. He might enjoy the evening without altering its natural course.

She was a woman on a date; she wanted to feel wanted. He knew how to do that.

"The truth is, I'd rather stay here with you." He bowed his head toward her like a gentleman. He was, at his best, a gentleman. She smiled, but it was a fainter smile than he had expected.

"I won't ask about work anymore, promise." She crossed herself as if entering a pew in church. Surely a nostalgic gesture from childhood, but he couldn't help sensing Geraldine beside them, or watching from above.

They ordered a tiramisu with two forks. And glasses of sherry. He was telling her about his wife. "She's been gone two years." He used his lines. They were true, and he performed them with the tinge of lingering grief. Who wanted to hear that he had been relieved when his wife died? Waking up every morning to her back turned away from him, her reminder that their twenty-five-year-old son, their only child, was gone. She wore their tragedy across her narrow lips; she couldn't get over that Kevin was dead and Morrison was still there, sitting at her kitchen table. His son had crashed his car on the way home from a club. Morrison could take blame for the driving and the drinking—he bought the car, believed parties were a young man's right—but his wife was the reason his heart numbed with such a singular ache. They had the one boy, and as his mother, she claimed sorrow as her right. What about Morrison's rights? She never answered him. It was too much, she said, and of course it was, so there they remained, apart and chained. He could not leave her. Not after Kevin died. He was the managing partner of Houghton, Park & Reed LLP, their divorce inconsistent with such responsibilities. And though he continued to believe her absence would rid him of his purgatory and leave him to the quieter corners of his loss, soon he would forget the idea of freedom from his wife.

He would forget because two partners rising through Labor & Litigation, smart women with good haircuts and Armani suits, followed up on a rumor. They talked to his former secretary, tracked down a paralegal. The affairs had ended conveniently—in natural succession, he wasn't a player—at each young woman's request. He assured these young women that he offered what he could, but he was loyal to his wife. They seemed to like him, love him sometimes, more for his clear allegiance. But the inquiries overlooked his decency. Then his wife got sick. A friend from law school, a loyal friend with his own habits, asked if he'd consider a judicial appointment. Morrison found the judiciary as dull as cardboard, but he recognized that at a critical juncture his career had catapulted, in the eyes of society, when it just as readily could have fumbled.

He found Geraldine in the City Hall secretarial pool. She worked as a substitute. She advertised her weekly Bible study on bulletin boards, and HR had kept her on lower pay and irregular hours for years. Geraldine said it was their concern about separation of church and state; they treated her as if she were Jehovah's Witness, which she was not, or a Hare Krishna disguised as a middle-aged woman. She did live by the Ten Commandments, and after Morrison's tumultuous last months at the firm, he told his wife he welcomed such stability. Not that Morrison and his wife acknowledged the change in his affairs, or his affairs, at the firm; she was the sort of Barnard woman who wouldn't, and they both respected her for it. She had her career in nonprofits, chairing luncheons for the children with cancer. She had Kevin, and when Kevin died, her sadness, and then her illness.

Morrison thought wearing the robe could fix any lingering habits as his wife's illness worsened, but he supposed it had been Geraldine sitting outside the Chamber with her God-given morality. Perhaps God had given him Geraldine so he would not stray when it mattered: she would inspire him to live up to his title, Honorable. But he believed in Geraldine more than he believed in God. She believed he was lonely. She wanted a woman to fill his heart till it shone from the inside, she said, as if he hadn't applied himself to the task.

It was raining the night he first drove Ventura Boulevard and found the bar in Van Nuys, the bar's dripping yellow sign half lit from a burned-out bulb. It was the day after his wife died, and what did he do with it. Morrison left his jacket and tie in the car, and within an hour followed a makeup artist back to her apartment. Later, he smelled the tinge of alcohol beneath the sweetness of her hair spray, the same bright and toxic clean that had surrounded his wife as she lay on the rented hospital bed in their bedroom. He came home and leaned over the empty bed, the slivers of guilt driving him there, and in his wife's lingering scent of shaded fern and medicines, he thought of the makeup artist. He would not see her again, but others followed. Dark pursuits, tendencies indulged. Geraldine reminded him what was his due every morning when she brought his coffee without the cream and sweetness he craved.

The restaurant seemed darker than he remembered. Waiters collected candles from the empty tables around them. Rebecca reached out for Morrison's hand. She smiled at him. Her fingers were warm now, and her polished nails a seashell pink. Geraldine sometimes decorated her nails with rainbows.

✳   ✳   ✳

"I don't drive," Rebecca said in the cab. "I used to, you know." She was relaxed from the drinks. A section of bleached-blond hair had fallen from her barrette and hung off the right side of her head. A flying buttress. His son had studied architecture. Morrison had his hand on her leg, the silk of her capri pants softer than he expected. He had offered to see her home, and she told him she lived in Burbank. He held her hand as the cab bounced its way east. Soon the driver would ask for an address. Streetlights flickered across Rebecca's face as she gazed out the window. She looked drained and forgotten, a naive midwesterner tarnished by years of smog, freeways, and strip malls. Her name wasn't Rebecca or Elaine. It was Carol or Mary. She could be standing in a light-filled kitchen sliding chopped carrots off a cutting board into a pot of chicken soup simmering on the stove; she'd listen to the radio, honest country songs, and nod to herself about the goodness she could make with her capable hands. Her husband, plain and well meaning, would walk through the front door after work and she would smile at the sound of his voice.

But she had imagined that there was something more for her outside of that place. And she had been pretty enough to try.

"I don't want to go home," she said, and nestled against his shoulder.

He paid for a room at the Hilton Universal City. From the window, in the distance, they could see the Universal Studios lagoon where Jaws gaped at tourists in tramcars. Red and white lights trailed past on freeways going north and south, east and west. Rebecca opened the minibar and cracked the caps on tiny bottles of whiskey as if she drank in hotels as a matter of course. She poured the whiskey into glasses left on a round tray above the television. She handed Morrison his drink, slid off her sandals, and sat beside him at the end of the bed. Morrison was loosening his tie, sliding the knot down, when she spoke.

"Last summer my eyes were bothering me. I could work and everything, but I wasn't making enough at the salon anyway. I had to give up my chair. I asked clients to come to the apartment, but I don't have the right sink and no one likes bending over for me to wash their hair. I didn't have money for the eye doctor—"

He kissed her. Her skin smelled like coconuts.

After a while he sensed her hesitate and she pulled away from him. She took a sip of her drink, then another until the glass was empty, and then her eyes fixed on his blue ones. Her eyes did not remind him of a basset hound's mild gaze, hers were dark.

"I didn't see well at night," she said. "My girlfriend got me a job at this restaurant in Sherman Oaks, waiting tables during lunch."

They hadn't turned on the lights or closed the shades. The lit-up billboards outside cast a haze over the room. Geraldine would not have arranged this date for him, and yet she had.

"I was driving back to my apartment from the restaurant, down a street with houses, a neighborhood. It was in the afternoon. There were sidewalks and basketball hoops on the garage doors, kids' bikes in the driveways. One of the houses had a silver Happy Birthday balloon tied to the mailbox."

She dabbed her nose with the back of her free hand. She let Morrison hold on to the other one. She looked somewhere to his left, out the window into the night.

She went on with it.

"I turned left at the corner and there was a little girl walking in the road right in front of my car," she said. "She just appeared. And I thought, I thought like I said it out loud, 'What is she doing there?' And then I hit her. It happened fast as lightning. Like it hadn't happened at all. I heard a woman scream and I kept going, I didn't stop. I drove away."

She spoke as if they were talking on the phone and he couldn't see her stricken face. Morrison felt the twinge in his chest, a little girl lying on asphalt.

"I thought someone would find me. I've been waiting for them, but they haven't come."

Rebecca, on the couch in her apartment with stained stucco ceilings, watching a closed door; he balanced the facts of the case, this loss, that one.

"I look at those sites sometimes, when I need a night out, you know, and I saw you were a judge. I've never seen a judge on those pages before. I thought you must be there for a reason, and I must've found you there for one." Her lip quivered and she turned from him.

Morrison squeezed her hand as if coincidence mattered, as if he sat beside her in a hotel room overlooking a mechanical shark lagoon for her reason.

"I decided if I'm going to tell someone, then this man is the one to hear me," Rebecca said. "I sent you a message and you asked me out and I knew it was right."

Blue mascara had streaked below her eyes.

"There is nothing right about this," he said.

She nodded. Her body shivered and he felt her sob, but she made the smallest sounds. He waited. The night wasn't any darker than it had been before, and eventually she quieted beside him.

Rebecca went into the bathroom, and Morrison lay down on the bed and closed his eyes. He was thinking about the little girl. But Rebecca's accident—it was an accident—didn't remind him of his son. His son had driven into a tree.

When he opened his eyes, Rebecca stood naked at the foot of the bed. She was lit from the city below, the cars driving the 101, the billboards advertising movies, jeans, and cologne. She looked younger, and quieter, and he realized that she had washed her face clean.

He was thinking about watching his son pitch in Little League. How Kevin's thin, weightless ten-year-old arm pulled back to hurl a baseball into the catcher's mitt. His little elbow bent up toward the sky. The silence of the crowd's attention. Morrison sat in the bleachers, knowing the pitch could spin wildly astray, leave his son alone on the mound, exposed. The boy was so young. Morrison waited for the pitch, stunned by such fragility. He waited for the release of his son's dangling arm, the snap of his wrist. He waited for what felt like a miracle. As the ball slung through the air, he felt for the chances that it might fly across home plate, that the hitter would miss or hold the bat steady and not swing at all. The ball carried something he didn't want to happen, something he worked against and couldn't stop from coming anyway.

"I'm not going to be here when you wake up and you're never going to find me," she said.

"I know," he said.

And she lay down beside him.

VENICE

*   *   *

The Collins family spent the last week of their European summer vacation in Venice, Italy, at an expensive hotel where Caroline's father did not allow her or her brother Robbie or her mother to eat lunch. Every morning the four Collinses ate from the breakfast buffet included with the room charge. There on the terrace overlooking the Venetian Lagoon, they asked for extra bread baskets and wrapped as many miniature versions of French pastries into their cloth napkins as they could. Robbie could hold two napkins stuffed with chocolate croissants and slide right out of the dining room. Robbie was thirteen years old, and Caroline fifteen. Caroline refused to smuggle pastries as she left the table and instead focused on the swing of her wavy golden hair down her back. She counted on her mother to arrange a peach, prunes, and one croissant beside her eyeliner and mascara on the dresser in the hotel room she shared with her brother. Her mother went along with her father's ideas and made the best of a situation, as did the kids. For example, Caroline and Robbie didn't ask why they could afford a fancy hotel but not lunch, or why they couldn't eat lunch someplace else. At noon or whenever they felt hungry, they obediently ate their stolen croissants. Her father was moody and they didn't want to fall on the side of his anger or, worse, provoke him. He was a businessman, in real estate; he paid the bills and he made the rules. When he proclaimed afternoon sundaes in place of lunch as the law of Venice, no one complained.

Besides, Caroline was thin and young enough not to care about eating too many ice cream sundaes. She was average height and wore that golden hair parted slightly toward the left and never tucked behind her ears. If she had a uniform that summer, it was high-waisted shorts and tank tops. Or short skirts. Or short sundresses with small floral prints. She knew how to dress for warm weather—she lived in Los Angeles, though not quite close enough to the beach; she had to fake balmy, sun-kissed California. Her arms were tan and because of their lean muscles, her favorite feature from the front. She had inherited the bumpy ridge of her father's nose and used the mascara and eyeliner to draw attention from it toward her gray-green eyes. She spent a lot of time looking in the mirror at her front and her back, and if there wasn't a mirror handy, thinking about what she looked like, while she trailed at least five steps behind her family around Europe.

Every day after breakfast, they toured Venice. They walked around some museum or square full of pigeons or an old stone building while her mother read to them from the Frommer's guide. Her mother believed their family could improve their essential natures with small bites of European history. Her mother wore her short-sleeved blouses tucked in, her Bermuda shorts belted, and bright white Keds for shoes. Her hair in a ponytail but her face a touch jowly, she looked like a competent babysitter who had overstayed their childhoods. Her mother's quest for mottled tapestries and the Gothic lancet arch fueled their entire three-week family vacation. As the sun rose and the smell of Venice—a saltwater scent tinged with exotic, baking garbage—wafted over them, they returned to the hotel pool for the hours of stifling midday heat. At the pool, they drank the free water and nibbled on their breakfast pastries. When they were starving and couldn't stand it any longer, they showered and dressed, and her father led them to a café he hoped was the same Venice café he'd last visited on his college graduation trip backpacking through Italy. He ordered a coffee sundae, which had been the café's signature dessert. Not an affogato, espresso served over vanilla, he insisted on a coffee sundae in a tall glass with syrup and whipped cream. He went on with this routine at each café, as if the dessert could eventually circle him back to a beginning when he was young, carefree, and, Caroline assumed, better looking.

So far, it had not.

"The place must be here," her father said. "Everything in Italy lasts a hundred years."

And the next afternoon he would try again.

Caroline occasionally tried to imagine her father as a young man in Venice. He had not yet met her mother and something had happened at this legendary café: he'd met a pretty girl? That was as much as she could imagine about her father. She sometimes pitied him his failed obsession. Despite his preoccupation with the café, he could not recall the name, the colors of the sign, or whether it existed on a corner or between other shops. She hadn't lived long enough to forget the details of what had been important to her. Caroline could believe her father had loved in Venice. Her father was twenty-three or -four then, his brittle hair softer and blond, his blue eyes curious instead of sharp. But she would never ask him why the café mattered. She waited for the scenario to play itself out. She surrendered to the momentum of her father's past, his diligent longing, as did her mother and brother. Each afternoon they tried a different café and insouciant waiters in thin cotton shirts misunderstood her father's description. Usually they brought him the espresso with scoops of vanilla. He complained; they shrugged.

Caroline would just as soon die when her father pointed to the ice cream and said, "Non, incorrecto," to the Italian waiter. She stared at her hands folded in her lap. She watched her breasts rise and fall with her breath, stretching against her cotton tank top. Once when she looked up, the waiter winked at her and she smiled as her parents looked flatly into their bowls.

She couldn't feign surprise at his attention. Walking the streets behind her parents, she heard the Italian men call to her with clicks of their tongues, like they did for the pretty dark-haired Italian women, only also not like them, because she was blond and American. She stood out. She waited for her father to reprimand them, or her mother to prod her father, and when they did not, her heart fluttered and her stomach turned a notch.

Caroline and the men were on their own.

❋   ❋   ❋

Every day she wore the same cover-up to the hotel pool. An indigo-blue sleeveless shirt that fell just below her bikini bottoms. It looked as if she might not wear anything underneath. One morning she was wearing the cover-up and carrying a *Vanity Fair* magazine in her straw tote bag down to the pool when a young, sandy-haired American man got on the elevator with her and Robbie. Robbie shifted to one corner of the small elevator and she the other as the man entered. Why, Robbie had complained, are the elevators in Europe smaller? It's not as if the people are. The man wore khakis and a collared shirt with the sleeves rolled up, and his tan forearms had the right amount of hair, not overly hairy like her father's arms. He wore Topsiders, boat shoes her father called them, with the emphasis on *boat* as if the shoes were worn by people who didn't know a thing about boats. Not that her father did, either. The Topsiders meant he was American. He nodded to her and Robbie, then took his place between them in the back of the elevator.

"Going to the pool?" the American said. He had friendly brown eyes.

"Yes," Caroline said.

"Do you think the sun is hotter here than at home?"

She liked his notion that she and he were from the same home, though dressed in boat shoes, he wasn't from Los Angeles.

Robbie crouched, preparing to jump for a few seconds of reversed gravity before the elevator reached the lobby. He was truly immature.

"Maybe, but they have umbrellas and cabanas and water spritzers for your face," Robbie said. "If you sit in a cabana, they bring your drinks on trays with cherries."

"Delicious," the man said, and Caroline couldn't help glancing over at him. He was looking right at her. She felt her face go red and looked down at her pink manicured toes.

Robbie jumped up then, and as the elevator stopped his feet thudded to the floor.

The doors opened. Robbie burst into the hotel lobby, but the man waited.

"Ladies first."

As Caroline stepped forward, she felt the brush of his arm, his arm hair, and then two of his fingers ran along her thigh, almost to the edge of her bikini. The touch was barely there, as if in walking out of the elevator she'd grazed his dangling arm. But her stomach and something lower lurched. She continued past the wall of gold-framed mirrors and then the wood-paneled concierge desk, and with each step the cover-up whispered against her bikini bottoms.

*   *   *

At noon, the Pool Man forbade the cannonball. I'm sorry, it's not a splashing pool is what the Pool Man said to Robbie in accented English. Caroline and Robbie called him the Pool Man because he walked around the pool in his black slacks like a sentry, and if a tanned European woman in a tiny swimsuit lay on a chaise, he stopped and offered her drinks. He snapped his fingers once, twice, and a waiter arrived with a sweating glass of water, then dashed away to fetch the woman a drink.

For perspective, Caroline and Robbie tried different chaises around the rectangular pool. They'd never stayed in a five-star hotel and looked out for its various angles. Robbie liked to visit the service entrance, where the hotel maids smoked and yammered on in Italian and let him bum cigarettes. He leaned against the building and tried to blow smoke rings and sometimes the maids smiled and laughed at him, as if he were their beloved, dim-witted nephew.

It was lunchtime and Robbie was hungry.

"This pool is boring as hell," he said.

Caroline wore her sunglasses low on her nose and waved her brother away.

"Why don't you go exploring," she said, like her mother would.

Robbie left for the service entrance and a cigarette, and Caroline went on pretending she did not see the American eating lunch on the hotel patio with a pastel-colored woman she assumed was his wife.

She wondered if the American had chosen to sit in that chair at that table to look out at Caroline lying here in her bikini, her skin wet from the pool and glistening. She smelled the sun's heat on her browning skin. She raised her sunglasses and spritzed her face with water—once, twice—like she'd seen the European women in the tiny swimsuits do. She closed her eyes and imagined the American watching her spritz.

❋   ❋   ❋

In the afternoon, they ate ice cream sundaes at another café that was not the one her father remembered from his first trip to Italy. Caroline looked across the table at her father's gray-flecked receding hair, the creases in his forehead, and his bristly eyebrows, and it was hard to believe he had once been her age. He was a stocky middle-aged man with a large nose and a distracted look in his eyes, as if you'd better not bother him while he thought about the repercussions of World War I.

"Can Robbie and I go exploring?" Caroline said, making fun of her mother this time, but her mother wasn't paying attention.

Her mother was dabbing sunscreen on her nose. She did not rub enough and her nose turned white. Her mother reminded Caroline of a plain brown sparrow pecking at the ground and twitching its wings with no one understanding or caring about these incessant movements except itself. The rest of them didn't say, Hey, your nose is white, or, You need to rub that in more. They let her mother look ridiculous.

Her mother glanced at her father, who stirred the milky melted ice cream in the bottom of his bowl. He'd eaten only half his sundae.

Her mother sighed and looked at her father's bowl on the table like she would a mud stain Robbie's soccer cleats had left in the carpet.

"I guess. Meet us here in an hour—watch out for pickpockets," she said.

Caroline and Robbie walked through a field of pigeons crossing St. Mark's Square and then down a narrow street toward a fountain. Robbie wore a T-shirt with *Nike* across the front, striped tube socks, and running shoes, as if he were the worst kind of tourist. A middle schooler from Ohio.

"Pickpockets are small-timers," he said.

"It can't be easy," Caroline said. "Sidling up to someone and reaching inside their clothes."

"Gross," Robbie said. "I'd rather snatch purses."

He studied the tourists and Italians milling around the open shops and street vendors as if he might snatch one.

When they reached the fountain, Caroline pulled a coin from her pocket, turned her back, and tossed the coin over her shoulder into the water. She wished for love, as always. And just like that, the American came to mind.

"By the way, I'm ditching you," she said, and left Robbie sitting on the ledge of the fountain, baiting a pigeon with a piece of his bitten-off fingernail.

She went exploring for Italian sandals. In Venice, her thin flip-flops, the accent to her casual LA chic, looked childish. For days, Caroline had admired sandals in the shop windows and on the dainty feet of Italian women. It wasn't what sandals the Italian women wore, the slides, slingbacks, and even gladiators, but how they wore them: effortlessly, yet with a coy invitation to admire them as they stepped across the stone pathways. Sandals were the next step, pun intended, toward her European/American, her cosmopolitan allure, and so she walked into a shoe shop. She found a pair with tan leather straps that crossed in the front and wrapped around the ankle and had the slightest heel. She handed over the credit card her mother had given her for emergencies. Despite or because of her father's efforts to teach her the value of money, Caroline cared a lot about what she could get with money when no one was around to stop her. She ignored price tags and exchange rates as if they involved complicated math, because the most successful defense with both her parents was ignorance.

She wore her new sandals out the store and around the streets, where she thought about how appealing she must look, with her golden hair and her bare shoulders and her sandals. At first, she felt the leather straps against the top of her foot and around the back, along her Achilles tendon, in the way a pair of tight jeans reminded her of her curvy backside. But soon the rubbing dug into skin and she lengthened her stride to reduce the pressure. Then she tried close, short steps as if she could remove the need to flex her feet against the taut leather. Perhaps she'd bought the wrong size, but she couldn't go back; her hour was nearly up. She resented her family for requiring her to report to them constantly. She'd have to make do with Band-Aids, or maybe the leather would stretch. Eventually. Her feet stung with blisters by the time she returned to the café, where her father read the *International Herald Tribune* and her mother Frommer's. Robbie arrived eating gelato from an enormous waffle cone.

"How much ice cream are you going to eat in one day?" her father said to Robbie, who ignored him.

"Did you know," her mother spoke to all or none of them, "there are eighty-five thousand square feet of mosaics in St. Mark's Basilica, enough to cover one and a half American football fields?"

Her father rustled the newspaper and Robbie licked a drip off his cone. "But Italians play soccer," Robbie said.

"True," her father said.

Her mother looked at the back of her father's newspaper as if she'd say something to the man hiding behind it but chose to bite her tongue instead. She turned to the next page in her guidebook.

No one noticed Caroline's sandals.

She loosened the leather buckle at her ankle and imagined the American admiring them. With the crossing straps, they looked like a bikini for your feet.

❋   ❋   ❋

The next morning, after another large breakfast, the Collins family met at the hotel boat dock for a trip to the Murano glass factory. Caroline wore a sundress with her new sandals and her hair wrapped into a twist secured against the wind of the boat with an army of bobby pins. She'd had a feeling about this day, ever since she'd found the American, or the American had found her. When she discovered him sitting beside the pastel-colored woman on the boat to the glass factory, she understood that the electric sensation running along her body, her skin almost on fire, was not anticipation, or longing, but instead her intuition signaling that something was in fact happening. To her.

The boats were bright wood and lacquered, with white or navy-blue bottoms. The boat drivers wore white pants and shirts; they had dark eyes and hair and held a woman's hand when she boarded or disembarked.

Caroline had gotten so used to holding hands with the boat drivers that she held out her hand before the boat driver reached for it.

"Buongiorno, beautiful," he said, and she smiled and said, "Buongiorno."

The American looked up as she and her mother sat behind him.

"Buongiorno," he said. "I'm Matt, and this is my wife, Annette."

Caroline's mother introduced their family. She asked where they were from.

"Michigan," Annette said. Her dull brown eyes were close together and squinted when she smiled. She had thin brown hair, a small nose, but a gorgeous complexion, porcelain skin. Caroline felt the pulsing itch of a zit above her own eyebrow. She resisted the urge to touch her forehead.

"I've heard the lakes in Michigan are charming," her mother said. She commented on regional delights as if the Frommer's guide had sunk into her bones.

"If you like mosquitoes," Matt said.

Annette put her arm around his shoulders, revealing a smudge of chalky deodorant under her hairless armpit.

"We love it," Annette said, and laughed and her eyes squinted at them. She squeezed Matt's arm, the arm that had touched Caroline.

Annette seemed *vapid*, one of Caroline's English comp vocabulary words.

The boat started. As they picked up speed, the wind whipped and Caroline held down her flapping sundress as best she could. They crossed the water in front of the hotel, an elegant building with four floors of guest room balconies. On the third floor, three pairs of Robbie's red plaid boxer shorts hung over a railing.

"Oh!" her mother said, looking back at the hotel as the boat drove farther away.

"What?" her father yelled over the motor.

Her mother pointed at the boxer shorts on the railing and shook her head.

"Listen," her father yelled, "you should praise the kid for doing his own laundry."

Robbie sat on the other side, waving his arms SOS at another boat too far away to notice.

Annette twirled her finger around the short hairs at the back of Matt's neck. This drove Caroline bananas. She stared and thought of a wave knocking Annette out of the boat and her drowning.

❋   ❋   ❋

The glass factory was a long gray one-story building on the island of Murano. An Italian woman in ballet slippers met them at the door and walked them through hallways with shelves of glass plates, bowls, cups, candlesticks, and whimsical animal figurines like a cat with a looping tail. The glass was thick and melted-looking, with bright colors running through it. Their group went mute and slow for the guide, as if touring a crypt. Caroline walked in front of the others and with each step felt for the edge of her sundress falling against her thighs. She did not hear Matt's voice, but occasionally Annette said, "Wow, look at that," demonstrating her lack of taste. In Michigan, Caroline was certain married women like Annette collected glass cats with looping tails.

For the grand finale, they gathered in a dimly lit room with a fire in the wall. A man in a black apron held a long metal pole with a glob of glass at the end. He worked the glass into the fire, heaving and rotating the pole. Just as the glass softened and drooped as if it could fall into the fire, he pulled it out and blew into the end of the pole while working the pole around and up and down, and soon the glass took the shape of something round and wide. Caroline liked the molten glass, its amoeba softness swaying above the flames, and how the man rotated and shifted the pole. Once the movement stopped, she was bored.

The glass hardened, and they peered at the end of the pole as they left the room.

"What is it?" Robbie said, looking at the glass stuck there like a Q-tip.

"Nothing," her father said. "It's a demonstration."

"They're going to melt it and make it into nothing again?" Robbie said.

"That's the point," her father said, and walked away.

In the glass factory store, her mother and Annette admired the fruit bowls. They picked up each fruit bowl and checked the bottom for the price even though they were the same size and style. Caroline was surprised Matt married a woman like her mother. It wasn't that she didn't like her mother, but her mother was the sort of woman she'd never want to become. A woman interested in glass bowls and Frommer's guides. A woman who ran a sponge over kitchen countertops, chasing crumbs after every meal. A woman who called volunteering in the local library a job. Maybe Matt and Annette were high school sweethearts, their families growing so close over the years that marriage was inevitable. Maybe Annette got pregnant and he had to marry her. They could have a baby waiting for them back in Michigan. But they were young; Annette could have had an abortion. Caroline walked outside and put on her sunglasses. Adult complications eventually bored her, too.

Her father and Robbie waited at the dock. A warm saltwater scent rose from the lagoon. As she watched them, it struck Caroline that the smell of Venice had become familiar. Robbie skipped rocks across the water while her father was talking. He had his hands in his pants pockets and leaned back and forth on his heels, which meant he was telling Robbie about his first trip to Venice. Caroline realized her father was a different person then, and when he told his stories he assumed this reminiscent pose she'd never seen before but found depressing.

She walked around the side of the glass factory, and there was Matt smoking and looking out at the water. She wondered whether Annette knew he smoked, and then decided his wife did not, or if she did, she wished he'd stop.

"I like your hair up," he said. "You look like a Modigliani."

"A what?" Her face flushed because she knew what he meant by it.

"His paintings of beautiful women. I think they're stunning."

He smiled then, but he didn't look at her. He looked out at the water. Men looked out at the water in Venice and thought about women. A gull bobbed on the surface and stretched its wings out to the sun. Caroline pulled at the skirt of her dress, suddenly smothering in the heat. The blisters on her ankles pulsed.

"I'll show you. Tomorrow," Matt said.

"Tomorrow?" She'd become a parrot.

He turned away from the lagoon and pointed the cigarette at her. There were beads of sweat along his hairline, that's where she focused, on the rise of his cowlick. He'd shaped his hair into a cresting wave that caused a catch in her throat.

"The Guggenheim museum, three o'clock."

She smiled without showing her teeth, mild flirting.

"Hey," Robbie yelled behind them. "It's time to go." He looked at her and then at Matt and back to her. He waved to Caroline to come on, to hurry up.

＊　　＊　　＊

She'd already visited the Guggenheim, a palazzo on the canal, with her parents. The walls were white and crammed with art. In the backyard, there were sculptures. During her mother's read-aloud from Frommer's, she learned Peggy Guggenheim was an American heiress who lived in this palace a long time ago with her modern art and Lhasa apso dogs. In the corner of the garden, there were two plaques above a square of gravel, one for Peggy and the other for her fourteen Lhasa apsos.

Peggy had boasted she had more than a thousand lovers, and Caroline believed her. An heiress sounded like a rich woman with many lovers.

When the time came to meet the American, Caroline ditched her family the same way she ditched school. She said she had a stomachache. After they'd left the hotel for their afternoon ice cream sundaes in the city, she showered and dressed and called the front desk for a boat taxi to the museum. She wore another sundress, short and loose and sleeveless, with her Italian sandals. The straps rubbed her blisters raw beneath the Band-Aids, but she paid no attention. In the boat with her hair whipping against her face, she felt like Peggy Guggenheim flying across the water to an Italian palace for a tryst with her lover.

At the museum, she wandered through the rooms of paintings—the Picassos and Pollocks and Mondrians—and then the gardens. She looked for the name Modigliani beside the paintings but couldn't find him; she never saw a painting of a real woman, either. Only lines and angles and misshapen bodies. She rubbed her sweaty palms against her sundress. She tried not to look at her watch.

She was looking for Matt, but when the time came, she didn't see him coming.

He found her in the sculpture garden.

"You look pretty," he said.

He looked right at her, like he had in the elevator. She couldn't help but look away, to the rounded bronze sculpture beside them, *Oval with Points*. Two sharpening points extended into the middle of the oval, almost touching.

"Where's the Modigliani?"

He laughed. "The truth is I didn't know whether they had one here or not. I just wanted to see you."

Caroline's head felt light and also funny, like she could pass out. She looked down so her hair fell across her face. Was he messing with her or not? One of her father's sayings came to mind, You're out of your league.

"Come on," he said, and took her hand. His hand felt warm and large in hers, encouraging. His palm soft and dry despite the heat. She couldn't feel the blisters on her feet, hadn't felt their sting since arriving at the museum. The lightness wasn't just in her head; she floated alongside him. She had anticipated ditching her family, arriving at the palazzo, and meeting the mysterious and handsome American, but she had no expectations about what would happen next.

From the sculpture garden, they walked into the palazzo. With her free hand, Caroline smoothed her hair, preparing for where they might pause and linger, and he would look at her more closely. At her naked arms and the ruffle along the scoop neck of her sundress. He turned and smiled at her as if he'd sensed her thought.

"Do you like the museum?" he said.

"It's nice here," she said, and when he raised his eyebrows she regretted her silly words. "I mean, I like the art."

"I'm not into paintings much myself," he said, glancing at the crowded walls. "But there's something to them together in one place. It's reassuring, like books in the library."

She tried to imagine him in a library and couldn't.

"That's so true," she said, and let her hair fall over her face.

He paused a moment and touched her hair, pushed it back behind her ear. She wondered if he was an easily happy person, or happy to be with her.

"You are hard not to notice." He kissed her hand and her heart or something else sank deep inside her chest.

"What do you mean?" she said.

"I could tell from the first time I saw you at the hotel, you weren't the typical girl."

"I don't know about that," she said.

"I do," he said, and squeezed her hand as he started walking. He was leading them somewhere.

They walked through another gallery, and she avoided eye contact with the tired, overheated men and women gazing at the walls with a vague satisfaction, as if they were supposed to understand what they could not. The museumgoers camouflaged her relationship with the American, such as it was. They passed through more tourists and then he led her up a stairway to a narrow hall, and his hand tightened around hers and he pulled her through a door labeled WC.

The WC was small and cramped and they stood so close her face brushed against the buttons of his shirt. When she looked up, he was smiling down at her, his pupils wide and shiny. Before she could wonder what would come next, he put his hands on her, slowly at first as he caressed her breasts and she would've said his expression looked almost peaceful, or dazed, but then he slid her sundress up her waist, and his fingers took over and moved with a certainty she couldn't question, they slipped inside her underwear, stroking, and his other hand touched her breasts, and she felt warm between her legs, warm for this man doing this to her body, and he freed up his hand long enough to undo his pants and lead her hand to his dick, and she stroked the strange flesh there but then she lost focus on her own pleasure and so did he, they both focused on him, his hand on her breast but her not feeling as good anymore, in fact, it almost hurt; he pressed her breast too hard signaling her to press harder on him, so she did. And then, out of nowhere, someone knocked on the door, loudly, like a teacher, and he pushed her hands off him and took up with himself, her standing to the side watching him do what she had never seen before, him hunched over the sink so as not to make a mess, and in a few seconds shooting into the porcelain bowl.

The person in the hallway knocked again.

"Un minuto," he yelled. He washed his hands in the sink and ran them through his hair, shaping his cowlick in the mirror until he was satisfied.

She bit her lip and it felt swollen, though he hadn't kissed her. She leaned against the wall beside the sink to avoid touching him as she pulled her bra and dress into place.

Footsteps in the hallway receded. The teacher gone.

"Do you need to wash up?" he said, his eyes on his face in the mirror.

"No," she said.

He listened at the door.

"They've left," he said. "I'll go out first. Wait a few minutes, and then you can."

He put a hand on her thigh. His fingers slipped along her underwear but only for a moment, skimming her again, like a pickpocket.

"Count to sixty twice," he said, and opened the door and left.

Caroline counted to thirty once.

The hallway was empty. She walked down the stairs and through the galleries of art and tourists. She did not expect him to wait for her, but she worried he might. He was not in the palazzo or the sculpture garden. The sandals cut into her blisters like knives. She unbuckled the straps around each ankle and walked barefoot through the gift shop to the exit, past a blown-up photograph of Peggy Guggenheim wearing metal earrings, thin paper clip sculptures that hung down to her shoulders. The earrings floated in space below her ears, and Caroline wondered if despite the dogs and lovers and money, she was looking at a lonely woman. She walked down the road to the water taxi stand, picking her way through the cobblestones, stopping to brush off loose pieces of gravel stuck to her feet. When a man clicked his tongue at her, she hurried toward an open taxi.

Robbie was waiting for her in the room with a pack of cigarettes. He wasn't surprised that she'd been out, or had returned barefoot with dirty feet and wouldn't speak to him until she'd showered. He didn't ask where she'd been. It was a relief Robbie looked at her as always, as if he didn't care, as if they weren't separate, but traveling together. It was their last night in Venice, the end of their European vacation. They sat outside on the balcony. As the August light faded over the water, he taught her to smoke the way the Italian maids had shown him that afternoon, head back and lips loose around a cigarette.

TOUCAN

*   *   *

The fall of their senior year in college, when they lived side by side in singles on the third floor of Little Hall, Lulu received an anonymous love letter. It was not her first love letter, but it was well written and included poetry. Carrie and Lulu read the words aloud to each other, ten times at least. *I think of you when I wake and when I go to bed and all the hours between.* The letter went on from there.

"Whoever wrote this, he's unimaginable, isn't he?" Lulu said, her eyes sparkling. She had soft brown eyes and full lips, and her auburn hair glistened in the sunlight, any light really. She prompted longing and unrest. Carrie, plump and dutiful, hovered at the edge of Lulu's glow. She craved brilliance as much as anyone.

Carrie could imagine Lulu's secret admirer. Tall and handsome. Misunderstood. He was known as the reliable, unassuming star of Princeton's heavyweight crew team, while he had passions incongruent to his jock identity. He'd watched Lulu Saunders for years, her carefree gorgeousness. Carrie could write their love story eyes closed, one hand tied behind her back. This young man—with the confidence of senior year, the pressure of his last chance—reached out to Lulu. She became the focus of his yearning, the woman he dreamed would celebrate his self-expression, his compassionate masculinity—strong and sensitive, handsome and humble.

Lulu couldn't think of a person on the crew team to match Carrie's description. Rowers were tall men with angular noses, broad chests, and long arms that swung from their shoulders like oars. Yet she sensed the greatness, the breadth, of this man's potential. What if one day they would marry? What if one day they had towheaded children together? The two friends felt as if they'd been drawn tingling and dazed into the center of a novel. September rains transformed the campus—the stone buildings and green lawns, the bushy-tailed squirrels and autumn trees—into crisp, vigorous forms. Another letter arrived, slipped into Lulu's book bag and again recited back and forth between Lulu and Carrie. It was Lulu's love affair, but the letters—ardent, sweet, and clever, which were the parts Carrie liked best—brought reverence into their friendship. They were the sole witnesses to a true love.

They kept the letters in a cookie tin, their list of possible admirers on top. Despite Carrie's interest in the crew team, Lulu had tired of athletes and scions. She had dated the Rockefeller and, later, the Firestone. She was interested in artists. In Slavic lit, she had been entangling herself with Andrew Despres. Andrew looked like a poet: tall and thin, with straight black hair that fell across his gray eyes. He'd grown up in New York, in the Village, a place of imaginary intelligentsia that intimidated and thrilled Carrie while Lulu took it in stride. But he wasn't a poet; he studied painting. Carrie had seen him at parties at Tiger Inn, standing in a corner with other smirking New Yorkers. A rumor claimed he lived in the city, commuted to school, and dated an actress.

*   *   *

"We've been waiting for you," Lulu's mother said when Carrie arrived at the Saunderses' beach house in Malibu. Carrie lied about traffic and missing a turn. Actually, she had dawdled and delayed and considered calling with an excuse. But not driving to see Lulu would be as disheartening as visiting her. It had been a year since college graduation, and Carrie had spent hers teaching eight-year-olds English in Costa Rica, alone. Failing to teach them, she was an earnest babysitter who peddled vocabulary flash cards. Lulu's family wouldn't know about that; no one did. Lulu had insisted Carrie stay the night in Malibu. There would be a dinner and she had something planned for afterward. Though Carrie had no idea what it was, she sensed the after-dinner program was the reason she'd been invited to the beach house. That, and to say goodbye. Lulu was ill.

The beach house was a narrow white stucco and glass rectangle wedged between others like it along the coast highway. There were three levels of ocean views, soft beige furniture, and pale hardwood floors. Carrie thought the house where she grew up an hour and a half away in Fullerton would fit on the first floor, while the clutter inside it, the couches, tables, dressers, mismatched chairs, televisions, would overflow onto the sand below. Mrs. Saunders called the beach house a cabana. She had Lulu's brown eyes and with her white blouse and linen skirt, a neutral elegance. Carrie had last seen her at commencement wearing a broad-brimmed sun hat with a peach silk bow; Lulu and Carrie had worn spaghetti-strap dresses and drank champagne on the lawn. Mrs. Saunders moved briskly around the cabana, which made her seem young, but her face was drawn, tired. Off the back of the house, a deck overlooked the gold sand and glittering sea. To the south, a jetty jutted into the water, the rocks hugging the beach into its crescent. Carrie found Lulu on the lower deck, reclining on a teak chaise as a hazy orange sun paused above the horizon and then dipped toward the ocean.

Lulu did not look like Lulu. The cancer medicines had bloated her face and torso, softened her. But when she stretched her legs across the chaise, Carrie recognized her delicate ankles and shapely calves. Carrie had lost weight in Costa Rica; still, when she sat down her jean shorts tightened around her thighs.

Lulu wore a Lakers baseball hat and aviator sunglasses, her lips thinned, her smile startlingly familiar.

"You're here!" she said, throwing her arms out to the fading yellow sunset. After that, they were talking like old friends. They overlooked the gap or falling-out or whatever had happened while Carrie lived in Costa Rica. Lulu had never written her back, never answered when Carrie called.

Mrs. Saunders had warned Carrie that conversations might lag or drift. The first tumor had appeared in a lymph node near Lulu's throat. Carrie pictured this tumor growing until Lulu couldn't breathe. It frightened Carrie. She watched Lulu's sunglasses and wondered whether Lulu was staring at her or watching the waves roll into the sand or the sun disappear.

On the beach in front of the house next door, two teenage girls, long hair and tan limbs—Lulu five years ago—chased each other toward the ocean. Lulu turned to follow their squeals, then looked away.

"Andrew would have drooled over those girls," she said. It was the first time either of them had mentioned his name.

＊　　＊　　＊

Carrie and Lulu had not solved the mystery of the anonymous letters on their own. The astonishing finale, or opening chapter, Carrie thought later, occurred when Andrew—because he was Lulu's admirer—appeared at Lulu's door, handed her the last letter, and asked her to dinner. That night, Lulu told her then-boyfriend, a gangly, earnest, and well-mannered all-American basketball player from Pennsylvania, that she was going out with Carrie; Carrie stayed in her room watching TV, and Lulu and Andrew fell in love.

"He is unimaginable," Lulu said the next morning. Her hair rumpled, she sat cross-legged on her bed, her face stunned by his adoration.

"What do you mean?" Carrie said. She could see the letters hurtling past her, their promises manifesting between Lulu and her lover. Carrie's boyfriends were brief, occasional, and felt as if she'd found them second-hand, cast off from some other woman's plans.

"He feels me in his heart," Lulu said. "It skips a little forward when I walk into a room, when he first sees me, or even if he thinks of me when I'm not there."

It was unheard of, until then, for a young man to speak of his heart. Sunlight shone through the window and flickered across dust in the air between them. Lulu and Carrie sat together quietly, observing its significance.

Lulu said she liked Andrew's unhurried approach to school and to life; she claimed that he made choices instead of following rules. When Carrie ran into Lulu and Andrew in the library or walking across the quad, Carrie did not know what to say to him. His gray eyes observed as if taking in details of her hair, her nose, her mouth for one of his paintings, but as far as she could tell, rarely engaged. Then he would smile, and she struggled to be witty, or useful, to yank him further forward. He answered her questions briefly, and if she went on, she felt a boredom come over him. Lulu didn't seem concerned about Andrew's reticence, and Carrie didn't think that she should. Once, at a reggae lawn party on a warm October afternoon, Andrew sat on a fence with his New Yorkers watching Lulu as she danced, her bare feet in the grass. Carrie wished a man might one day look at her with the same concentration.

Lulu and Carrie planned to teach English in Costa Rica after graduation, and there was talk that Andrew might join them, as if this news would excite Carrie as well. Costa Rica had been Lulu's idea. She and Carrie were almost fluent in Spanish; Carrie had grown up around her father's construction crew and Lulu had a housekeeper. But Carrie thought she should get a job. She searched the white notebooks on the job listings shelves at Career Services. She flipped through Broadcasting, Journalism, Finance, and Nonprofit as if one of their neatly typed pages, smudged and softened on the edges by fingerprints like hers, might identify her pursuit. None spoke up. Their fluid descriptions seemed written for ambition, for a hardness that Carrie couldn't muster. In the end, she decided Lulu's Costa Rica offered a line for her résumé. She was wary of teaching—standing in front of a classroom of rabid or, worse, dull nine-year-olds—but with Lulu she could manage. They would share an apartment, plan their lessons together, and on the weekends hike dirt paths to Mayan temples. This is it, Lulu had said when they applied for the year abroad, our chance to have an adventure. No one else is going to Costa Rica. Just us, together.

Carrie had to take herself out of Costa Rica to make room for Andrew.

Then in January Lulu came down with a strange flu; the doctors ran tests and found a tumor on the side of her neck.

It was Andrew who flew back to California with Lulu for treatments that winter. The cure rate for her kind of cancer, Lulu explained when she returned in the early spring wearing a gift from Andrew's mother—an Hermès scarf with bright geometric patterns wrapped around her beautiful bald head—was almost ninety percent. The college was understanding, helped Lulu make up her credits. After graduation, Lulu and Andrew returned to California and Carrie flew to Costa Rica to teach summer classes until the school year started. She supposed she'd felt loyal to Lulu's adventure. And where else would she go, where else could she go?

❋   ❋   ❋

"Gillespie wrote me that she'd seen him in New York," Carrie said on the beach house deck. Casual, as if they were talking about someone else's ex-boyfriend.

"Gillespie would. She probably wrote everyone," Lulu said. "I was surprised you didn't call."

Lulu looked at Carrie then, and Carrie shook her head at her own lapse.

"I should've. I meant to," Carrie said. "I lost track, I'm sorry."

"He's dating a model," Lulu said, and when she didn't laugh at the ridiculousness of models, Carrie realized that Andrew had, perhaps, dumped Lulu. She should have called.

The sliding glass door opened and as if summoned, Debra and Kristen walked out to the deck. Earlier, Carrie had found Lulu's new best friends whispering to each other in the kitchen while they sliced fruit and wrinkly kale for Lulu's smoothie.

Kristen and Lulu had gone to high school together, and Lulu met Debra in a support group at the hospital. Debra, a decade older than Lulu, had a husband and kids and was cured. Lulu wore her baseball hat over a monotone wig; Debra had her own hair and it was streaked with gold strands. Despite the sun-kissed salon hair and slim waist, Debra reminded Carrie of the peroxide-blond teenage girls Carrie had avoided in Fullerton, bulging flesh below crop tops, heavy doses of mascara, frosted pink lipstick. When Debra eyed Carrie with distrust, or disinterest, Carrie imagined her sweating in the gym, taming her body's natural curves. It seemed only Carrie sensed she had assimilated from somewhere else.

Kristen was also blond, Scandinavian, her face as placid as watching golf on TV. She wore a bikini top and surf shorts low on her hips. She would tell not-funny-enough stories about ex-boyfriends with crisp names like Bret, Nick, and Jake. But Lulu would laugh. As soon as she met Lulu's new friends, Carrie regretted the ragged edges of her jean shorts and the sleeveless blouse she left unbuttoned at the bottom. She must look flimsy in her clothes.

Debra sat down at the end of Lulu's chaise and began to massage her feet.

"We're talking about Andrew's girlfriend," Lulu said.

"The Wonder-fucking-bra model," Debra said.

"She's a lingerie model? You've got to be kidding," Carrie said.

"No, why would I?" Debra said, her stare cutting Carrie out of the fold.

"Underwear, it's so tacky," Carrie said.

She was relieved when Debra laughed. "And Andrew is such a tactful asshole!"

Lulu leaned her head back on the chaise. Her aviators rolled toward Debra. "My mom hates swearing," she said.

"Well, then I better close the fucking door," Debra said. She got up and pulled the sliding glass door shut.

Kristen sat down beside Carrie.

"Can you stay for dinner?" Kristen said.

"She's spending the night," Lulu said. And Carrie wondered if she should have made an excuse to decline that invitation.

"I really like your bird sculpture," Kristen said. On Carrie's walk through the beach house, she had noticed her clay toucan on the nightstand in the room where Lulu slept. Carrie had made the toucan in high school. He was almost a foot tall, with a glazed white belly, shiny black tail feathers, and an orange beak. She sent him to Lulu last week when she heard the news. The toucan on the nightstand gave her hope, for what she wasn't sure—admission? Relevance?

"Are you an artist?" Kristen said. Her willing nature tired Carrie. In college, she had played Kristen's role.

"Not really," Carrie said. She looked over at Lulu. Her eyes were closed. Carrie wondered if her neck hurt.

"Have you seen Lulu's pottery?" Kristen asked.

"She's amazing on the pottery wheel," Debra said.

Kristen leaned toward Carrie and lowered her voice. She had noticed Lulu resting.

"It's been calming for us, the pottery class," Kristen said.

"I just made the one bird," Carrie said.

"What is it, a puffin?" Debra said.

"A toucan," Lulu said, her eyes still closed. "Carrie found out I was dying and she sent me her toucan. And I love him."

❋   ❋   ❋

When Carrie returned from Costa Rica, she had called Lulu right away. Like a reflex she had to exercise, or curiosity, or a need to witness what had moved on without her. After she left two messages, Mrs. Saunders called back with the shocking news. Lulu's cancer had recurred. She was spending *her months*, Mrs. Saunders said—and Carrie understood she meant Lulu's last months—at their beach house in Malibu.

Carrie lay on her bed cornered by the news, her lateness and its inevitability. No one had thought to summon her from Costa Rica. Or it had been her responsibility to continue writing her sick friend, no matter the response. *Lulu was dying.* Carrie felt an urgency to act, to compensate for her neglect. To send Lulu something. She wanted more than a gesture; buying a gift felt insincere, a token from the living. She searched her bedroom shelves: the half-burned candles, worn stuffed animals, books she no longer wanted to read, then in the corner, the orange beak of the toucan she had sculpted. Everything else she made that semester—the coil pots, bowls, and mugs with sturdy handles—exploded in the kiln. The toucan was all she had left.

Carrie held the toucan in her bedroom and recalled the moist iron scent of wet clay. She felt the grooves, the lines running parallel and merging, like feathers. For a model, she had studied a *National Geographic* picture of a toucan perched on a branch in a green rain forest, maybe in Costa Rica. She dipped her fingers into a bowl of water and molded the curve of its body. She pressed the block of cold clay gently until the figure emerged, as if it were a real bird with a proud breast and resting wings. Then she shaped a beak and sculpted eyes with tiny cuts into the surface. She etched tail feathers with arcing strokes, over and over until the texture emerged. She chose to sculpt a toucan for the beak, oversized and orange, set off by the bird's black-and-white tuxedo feathers, demanding attention: Look at me.

The toucan had endured Carrie's bad luck with the kiln, triumphed against the odds, but it would not reverse Lulu's fate. An essence of herself is what Carrie wanted to send. The time pressing and carving the slab of clay into a bird was meditative, pure. Carrie felt the most of herself, enlisted completely in the calm, thrilling pleasure of what she could do with her hands, what she could imagine into being. She included a note: *Thinking of you—Love always, Carrie*. She debated the *always*, whether it sounded insistent or saccharine. But she wanted to apologize for Lulu's misfortune, that death could occur for no reason, when it shouldn't, and she meant her *always* to say *I'm sorry this happened to you*.

Lulu called. "He's handsome," she said. "Is he a special parrot?"

"A toucan," Carrie said, having never considered whether the toucan was male or female and wondering whether she should have. And then Lulu invited her for the weekend at the beach.

*   *   *

They drove to an American/Italian restaurant for dinner, and when Lulu refused to sit at the head of the table, Mrs. Saunders nudged Carrie to sit there instead. With her tight smile and choker of pink pearls, Mrs. Saunders maintained a certain decorum over the evening. She glanced at Lulu, sipped her dry martini, glanced at Lulu, sipped her martini. She asked Carrie questions about Costa Rica, which Carrie answered blandly, as if she'd recently read a travel brochure about the place.

The table of women felt lonely, off balance. They spoke quietly, with anticipation; Carrie considered they were waiting for the important actors to show up, like Jesus or the grim reaper. Lulu's father and brother had gone on a fishing trip for the weekend. They needed a break, Mrs. Saunders said, as if they belonged to a weaker sex. Carrie had never seen Lulu without a man of some kind in orbit. Debra talked about her children eating dirt in the yard and swinging their cat in a pillowcase. Kristen and Lulu split the salmon and held hands as if they shared one cardiovascular system, passing blood through tightly woven fingers. Carrie eyed their entwined knuckles, the matching gold signet rings on their pinkies, and dreaded spending the night. She hoped they wouldn't stay up late talking. She used to with Lulu, imagining their adult lives. The men they would meet, the city streets they'd walk on bright, clear mornings, and there were other scenes in this montage, but somehow Carrie had forgotten the rest of their dreams.

They had fudge brownie sundaes for dessert. Debra ordered one for each of them without asking, as if that's what they always did. Mounds of vanilla dripping with sauce, hunks of brownie underneath. Carrie had gotten through her roasted chicken. She poked at her ice cream.

Kristen dug a cavern in the side of her dessert.

"It's Lulu's favorite," she said.

Lulu dabbed a spoon into the whipped cream on the top. Her makeup couldn't cover the darkness under her eyes. She ate her whipped cream and smiled as if it brought her a satisfaction. They each had a role to play.

"Mine too," Carrie said. And she gorged on her dessert until the bowl was empty.

＊　　＊　　＊

Carrie had received one postcard from Lulu. It arrived her first month in Quesada, Costa Rica. *MISS YOU!!!! XOXO, L.* And then nothing more. Carrie lived alone on a busy, potholed street above a restaurant that also served as a market, selling baskets of plantains and strange foods in cartons and cans. If she opened her window, she could smell the fruit ripening in the late afternoon sun and hear the restaurant television blare soccer matches in bursts of Spanish. In the distance, she could see the green mountains surrounding the lake that she had not yet visited because she worried she'd get lost on the bus ride out of town. She wrote Lulu letters about the boys and girls in her class, their electric laughter and eager, "Please, Missus, please Missus!" She didn't describe her paralyzing stage fright the first week, which led to constant, rambunctious challenges to her authority, or that she was quiet with the other teachers, who came and went from the school every month, so there were always unfamiliar American faces, acquaintances too brief for companionship. The adventure had not turned out right, or she turned out not to like adventure.

Those first months in her cockroach-sharing apartment in Costa Rica she had dialed the Saunderses' house in Brentwood each week and left messages until she couldn't leave any more. After scribbling and posting airmail envelopes to Lulu and receiving nothing in return, Carrie tossed the photo she'd tacked up on the wall of her and Lulu with their arms around each other. They were wearing sweaters and standing in the snow, which made no sense in the humidity of her flat. Then Carrie went back to watching *Dynasty* reruns dubbed in Spanish.

During Quesada's rainy season, relentless days of downpour, word reached Central America that Andrew had left California and moved back to New York. Gillespie's letter. At Princeton, Susan Gillespie had tried to wedge Carrie from Lulu, slip into her spot by meeting Lulu for coffee and borrowing ratty T-shirts and Levi's that made up Lulu's style at school. Gillespie was a horsey girl from New Jersey—she even rode horses—and worked as a paralegal at a big firm; soon she'd be starting law school. Carrie appreciated Gillespie's letters to Costa Rica, no matter what she said in them.

Carrie had already stopped writing Lulu, and she didn't think to then.

From the silence, and now Andrew's departure, she understood that Lulu had finished her treatments, and with her illness completed, a page had been turned. Carrie was easily overlooked. She and Lulu were separated by months and months, and countries spread out between them. She remembered reading Andrew's letters with Lulu, the two of them sitting on Lulu's bed with their plastic cups of seven-dollar chardonnay, reciting lines as if under a spell. She'd seen Lulu's passions subside before, as they had for the basketball player from Pennsylvania. Or not like him, because Andrew was different. Carrie imagined Lulu's hair had grown out thick and glossy, and she had found another Adonis, a blue-eyed surfer. She had lost interest in poets and artists.

᎗ ᎗ ᎗

When they returned to the beach house, it was Carrie who settled Lulu under blankets on a chaise close to the firepit. Mrs. Saunders had driven back to the other house. Before leaving, she hugged Lulu on the front porch. Mrs. Saunders was a few inches shorter than Lulu, but she clasped her daughter to her chest and gently rocked her back and forth. Carrie looked away.

The firepit ignited with a gas switch, then flickered silent orange and blue flames. In the dark, it was a large black glowing cauldron. Lulu held a cardboard box on her lap. Kristen and Debra hovered, and Carrie waited for the something serious that had been planned.

"Are you sure, sweetie?" Kristen said to Lulu. She was more sensitive than Carrie. A better friend.

Lulu looked at Carrie. "I've got everything of Andrew's in here. We're going to burn it."

"May his dick rot in hell," Debra said. Carrie wondered if she talked this way in front of her kids. She seemed like a woman who would.

Lulu wrapped her arms around the edges of the box. Her head bent forward as she stared at the contents, and her eyes were wet, but she didn't cry. She pulled out a worn T-shirt and smelled it. Then she balled up the shirt and tossed it in the fire. The flames whooshed a blazing yellow. The shirt combusted in a swirl of smoke and sparks.

Debra whooped. Lulu handed her another shirt from the box, and Debra dropped it in the fire. Kristen threw in plaid boxers. Lulu held a stack of photos; she tossed one at the flames, watched as its edges curled, melted, and then ignited. Lulu hesitated at the next picture. She squinted at it, then handed the photos to Kristen.

"Just throw them in," she said.

Kristen leaned over the fire and dropped the photos; her skinny arm recoiled as if she'd burned herself.

"I'm alright," she said quietly, but no one other than Carrie noticed. Lulu was digging through the box; Debra had her hand out for more.

Restaurant napkins, concert tickets, a woven rope bracelet, a stuffed banana amusement park prize, a lock of dark hair, champagne corks, an *I heart Wildwood, New Jersey* bumper sticker. The fire absorbed every piece of evidence they threw into its jittering flames. Carrie hung back and waited for the strange ritual to end. They carried on as if they'd forgotten her. After they burned a hooded sweatshirt into a cloud of black ashes, Debra's shouts faded and it seemed the box must be empty. But then Lulu reached into the box and brought out several loose notebook pages. She held them out to Carrie.

Andrew's secret admirer letters were each no more than a page in length, his black handwriting angled and narrow across the lined paper. He left a few scratch-outs, words reconsidered, and Carrie remembered appreciating the authenticity. She took the letters from Lulu, nodding that she understood the significance of her appointment. The letters slipped from Lulu's fingers as if she could barely hold on to them.

Carrie didn't want to be the one who burned the letters. She had the sense that none of them, other than Debra, were behaving as they would ten years from now.

"These are all the letters he wrote you?" Carrie said.

"Yes."

Carrie didn't move. In the firepit, flames licked at the air.

Kristen sat on Lulu's chaise, roosting there in her slim jeans and tank top.

"She's thought about it and this is what she wants," Kristen said.

"I don't need an interpreter," Carrie said.

"They're my letters," Lulu said.

Debra reached out her hand. "Give them to me. I'll do it."

Carrie held the notebook pages as the women watched her. Whoever he was, Andrew had revealed a love affair, its freedom and exhilaration. She craved his hopefulness instead of this night on the deck burning boxers and T-shirts as if they offered a cleansing, which they could not. They were clothes a man once wore. Carrie felt the darkness at her back and, down at the beach, the waves sliding and breaking against the sand. She wanted proof of life, even if it was another woman's, even if Lulu was dying and had no more use for her lover, especially then. Though as she held the college-ruled pages, she worried their magic came from the shelter of a campus, the rhythm of immature days. But she had to save the letters while she could. At twenty-three, she sensed youth disappearing with a ruthless pace. The time the letters marked might have been her best days. Her proximity to a true love. Her closest friendship with Lulu, or perhaps anyone.

"I'll keep them tonight," she said. "Tomorrow you can burn them or tear them up or throw them in the ocean."

"Not your decision," Debra said.

"You're ruining Lulu's plans," Kristen said.

Lulu pushed herself forward on her chaise. She pinched the bridge of her nose. She had never liked conflict, not in front of her. She hadn't minded if girls and boys had fought one another for her favor while she pretended she loved them all just as much. Oh, how Carrie had loved her role as favorite.

"I don't want it to end like this," Lulu said.

"Nothing's ending," Debra said. "Every moment has its own beginning."

"I don't know what that means," Lulu said. "It sounds like some bullshit from group."

Kristen smoothed the blanket over Lulu's feet.

"She was just trying to—" Kristen said, but Lulu waved a hand at her.

"I want to say something," she said.

Lulu looked at Carrie then, and it was like they had never met. Lulu's face swelled along her jawline while her cheeks were sunken to the bone. Her brown eyes shone black in the firelight, despair settled in the dark circles beneath them. When Mrs. Saunders hugged Lulu on the porch, Carrie had felt loss rear up and spread its tentacles. Her mother had gently caressed Lulu's back as if she were still a child. The rest of the time they would stave it off, Mrs. Saunders, Kristen, Debra, and Lulu, divert its presence with the sun and the beach, the blue ocean and their scripted conversations. If Carrie had reached Lulu sooner, if she hadn't disappeared in Costa Rica, she could have fallen in line with them. Instead, she'd become warden of letters, fragments from the past where Lulu was gorgeous and divine.

Lulu nodded at Carrie as if they had an agreement.

"I'm tired, I need to go to bed," Lulu said. "And Carrie's right."

The next morning Carrie drove back to her parents' house in Fullerton, and the morning after that Lulu went into the hospital. They held her funeral five days later.

❋   ❋   ❋

At the memorial service, the minister spoke of Lulu's dear friends who had suspended work and time with their families to spend these last months with her. *These brave women gave their love, their laughter, their enduring presence when she needed it most.* He asked them to stand. Kristen and Debra rose from the pew in front of Carrie. They were the ones who slept on the floor by Lulu's bed at the beach house. Carrie spent her one night on the living room couch, counting the minutes, thinking about the toucan keeping watch on Lulu's nightstand.

After the service, Carrie walked through the reception at the Saunderses' house, looking for Andrew. She had seen him outside the church. Alone in his dark suit, an East Coast suit, he was easy to find among the pastel dresses and linen sports coats. Mrs. Saunders had requested summer attire. Carrie hadn't had the nerve to speak with him then. Kristen sat on the living room couch, accepting condolences in place of Mrs. Saunders, who wandered from room to room, adjusting the bouquets of pink peonies her daughter had loved. Lulu's black and white portrait, her brilliant smile, leaned on an easel by the empty stone fireplace.

Mr. Saunders stood in the kitchen, speaking solemnly with several older men. They looked at the floor as they spoke. Lulu's brother sat outside by the pool with his own group of straight-faced boys nudging loose pebbles from the landscaped planters with their shoes. Inside, a harp played in the corner while a gray-haired woman leaned over the buffet table and picked at a cheese plate with her fingers. Carrie's college friends had already left. She and Gillespie had cried for a few minutes together, it felt almost natural. After a while people didn't know what to say, the hushed conversations around her sounded restless. She stopped in the entryway next to Debra, who was talking to her husband on the phone. "No, hon," Debra said. "It's not over yet. I left pasta in the fridge for you and the kids."

Carrie found Andrew on the back patio, leaning against a Mediterranean column. In the heat, his skin was pasty, his black hair limp.

"I came in this morning on the red-eye," he said. "Mrs. Saunders said it would be alright."

Carrie had been relieved to see him sitting in the back of the church.

"Did you see her parents yet?" Carrie said.

Andrew looked at the peeling trunk of a eucalyptus tree hanging over the lawn. "I did," he said.

"Costa Rica was awful. I hated it," she said.

Andrew's gray eyes settled on her face. She wondered what they picked out: her freckled nose, narrow-set green eyes, the chapped lips. She had lost weight since college; her stomach couldn't handle the spices in Costa Rica. And she was tan.

"Why didn't you come home, then?" he said.

"I don't know," she said. Every night she had crawled into bed with plans to leave, but when the morning sun blazed through her shadeless apartment windows, she felt obligated to see her choice through. Princeton loomed over her, its expectation that she turn out worthy. Carrie, weighed down by her potential, when Lulu's had been taken.

Andrew loosened his tie and the top buttons of his dress shirt.

"I don't think I can stay here much longer," he said.

❋   ❋   ❋

It was early afternoon, but they drove to the coast and found a bar open by the pier, and then a motel with vacancies next door. A watercolor of a sailboat hung at the foot of the bed, and there were anchors on the faded blue wallpaper. Outside, boats floated in the marina.

Andrew waited to kiss her until they were in the room. He wasn't tentative or questioning, nor did she feel the two of them in a motel room had been part of his plan. She realized that she had been wrong about Andrew. He wasn't detached; he was self-contained. She liked the smell of his skin. As his hand slipped beneath her dress, she considered whether he was too good for Lulu and then she considered what too good meant, whether one person could be worthier or more valuable than another. She was thankful for the drinks at the bar, while wondering if later she might regret them and the opportunity they had created but knowing she wouldn't. If she was learning anything in sleeping with her dead ex–best friend's ex-boyfriend, it was something about the physical at the expense of everything else. She slipped off her sandals. He lifted her dress over her head. She unbuttoned his shirt and felt he was right to stay so close; the touch of his chest and stomach and hips, his mouth against hers, his hands on her back, meant they could only go forward. He kicked off his suit pants, left them on the blue carpet, and led her to the bed. He kissed her neck and then her breasts, and she felt her body provide a belonging. She felt the closest to Lulu, as if she and Lulu were of the same matter.

She considered whether she had wanted Andrew in this way, for herself, since the memorial service, or long before, when she sat in the dorm room with Lulu and read his first letters. But she hadn't. She hadn't thought about making love, if that's what they were doing. Reading the letters, she'd wanted to be his subject, the girl who turned his heart. In the bar, she had waited beside him, watched the condensation drip down her glass; she had let the silence come and go, until he needed her, and she would go as far as he would take her, she never thought of stopping him, of coming to her senses. She thought that until this moment she hadn't felt herself clearly since childhood, since before she could remember she had been looking at herself from a distance.

Carrie reached her arm from the covers and brushed the hair from Andrew's forehead. His eyes were fixed on the sailboat drifting in the painting.

"She hated me, didn't she," he said.

"I don't know," Carrie said.

"I don't believe you," he said.

"Did you write letters to Virginia?" Carrie asked. Virginia, who modeled in swimsuit catalogs, not lingerie.

"No," he said. His breaths shortened. Carrie sensed that he had.

"Do you copy the sentences from books?" Carrie hadn't thought of him plagiarizing before—when she and Lulu had studied every phrase. They had such belief in Andrew. The letters had been lyrical, without gushing; they were sensitive and raw. She wanted him to speak the words, to her, so she could feel their sway.

"I've got to leave for the airport soon," he said. He made no motion to rise.

Carrie was silent, waiting.

"Why did you leave her?" she said.

Andrew stared at the painted sailboat, its sails unfurled over a flat ocean.

"You went back to New York," she said.

"I couldn't be there any longer," he said.

"Why not?"

"I tried," he said. "It's not like I didn't try to stay."

"She wanted me to burn your letters, but I couldn't."

He lay still beside her.

"You don't need to tell me everything," he said.

If he cried then, Carrie couldn't tell. She didn't want to look at him.

✻ ✻ ✻

In the fall, Carrie temped as a receptionist while she finished her law school applications. She lived at home. Her parents mostly left her alone. They didn't ask questions when she cleared out her bedroom, dumped the items from her shelves into trash bags, and drove her childhood to Goodwill. She kept her bedroom as empty as the beach house, her clothes in drawers, LSAT study guides in a backpack beside her desk.

One day Carrie received a package from Mrs. Saunders. *Lulu wanted you to have these.* There was a large envelope and a small present wrapped in tissue paper. Lulu had written *Carrie* across the envelope.

After Kristen and Debra took Lulu in for bed and Carrie turned off the fire on the deck, she had read Andrew's letters. She couldn't not read them. She skimmed the lines like an embarrassed intruder opening drawers while Lulu slept on the other side of the living room wall. Andrew's words felt old, or she felt old reading them. They recalled a liveliness in her past.

She was most comforted by the handwriting, the intent held in the pen sliding across those ruled lines. When she had read the letters with Lulu, the pages held the unknown, the love affair itself. Now a relationship had come and gone. The next morning, she left the letters on Lulu's nightstand, under the toucan. She picked up the toucan and the bird felt heavy in her hands, like a rock. The etched lines more amateur than she remembered.

Carrie sat on her bed and opened the envelope from Lulu. She found Andrew's letters folded as she had left them. Behind the letters she found more, ten pages of his sloped scrawl. These were not carefully composed; he repeated sentences from one day or week to the next, pleading with Lulu to listen. They were dated, with the time. Several marked as two or three in the morning, after Andrew and Lulu had been on the phone. He swore he was taking a cab to the airport and flying back to California. He said it hurt more to be sent away than to be with her until the end. She wasn't saving him, he didn't know where she'd gotten the idea that one of them could be saved. She didn't have the right. But it seemed that she had. *I can make my own choices, and I choose you.* How had she kept him away? What had she not wanted him to see in her, in her dying? When had he given up and found the other girl? Is that when Lulu understood her mistake? She had not known until then. She wouldn't try to call him back, the farthest she could reach was to set their relics on fire, destroy what she believed he had already erased.

Carrie unwrapped the present slowly.

It was a picture frame with a photograph of Lulu and Carrie from college, their arms around each other under Blair Arch. The same photograph Carrie had thrown away in Costa Rica, as if Lulu had known she'd lost it. They wore wool fisherman sweaters, jeans, and boots, and stood on a blanket of snow. The snow was three or four inches thick at most, but it looked luxurious. Carrie and Lulu had pink cheeks and bits of white in their hair. They had just carved angels on the lawn, flying their arms and legs across the snow as they stared up into a blue sky. Carrie remembered the cold on her back, the carelessness of lying on the lawn in the middle of winter.

ORACLE

* * *

Alan's wife woke him up in the night. She squeezed his shoulder and said, "Did you hear that?"

"How could I?" he said, his voice sloggy and his mouth dry as he slept on his back, his lips parted to the heavens. He could've been snoring. He had been snoring. "I was asleep."

"I heard a noise," his wife said.

They lay still, listening in the dark. Their bedroom was on the second floor at the end of a hallway. They lived in a large house in Bel Air, not obscene, but if his wife called to him from the kitchen, he often pretended he didn't hear her. On a sunny Los Angeles afternoon, tourists in the Star Maps Tour vans could point at their green hedges, their iron gate, and call it a mansion. They had lived here for ten years. Happily. He made and returned calls from his office down on Wilshire Boulevard, and she looked out for their overall well-being: food, clothing, decorating and redecorating the house. They went out to dinner with friends a couple times a week; they had people over for drinks on the terrace, a stone patio bordered with yellow rosebushes, but his wife called it the terrace. She understood nomenclature. Alan went along with his wife's preferences and she would say that she catered to him. She bought him blue suede loafers and designer T-shirts with large initials on the front or back that were not his, and he wore them even when they made him feel stupid. Such agreeableness was the cast of their marriage.

The silent house waited with them in the dark, and soon enough, a thump sounded downstairs.

"There's someone down there," his wife said, her voice hushed. She sat up in bed and looked at him as if he should go down there, too. He had no impulse to get out of bed and tiptoe downstairs in his pajamas.

Then, another thump. A slow-moving elephant on the first floor.

If they had a phone, they could call the police, but they'd left their cell phones downstairs, with the burglar. No one had landlines anymore; what was the point? This was the point.

"If we had a phone," he said, "we could call the police." He pulled the bedcovers to his chin.

His wife believed in radiation from cell towers and Wi-Fi and electromagnetic fields. She recited articles about glioblastomas. She called their bedroom a "clean air zone." Technology will be the end of us, she said.

His wife might be an oracle, the kind that sets you up to die by pretending to save you.

"What if they come for us," she said, their thoughts on the same trajectory. She swung her bare feet to the rug and crept to the door.

"For God's sake," Alan said. "Don't—"

"It's locked," she said, and came back to bed.

His wife was a decade younger than Alan, with bright blond hair, blue eyes, and pouty lips. She reminded him of a Siamese cat, beautiful, enigmatic, and loud. She'd explained early on in his courtship that she didn't have a daddy complex, her curiosity about men her age had expired. He'd been drawn to her pragmatism; and when she was impractical, he respected her certainty. But she could be oblivious of her effect on people, her slinky blouses. What if these men followed her home from the parking lot at Saks? What if they had plans beyond clearing out his computers and television and wine cellar, assuming they knew wine? He had never seen her looks as a liability.

It was up to him to protect her.

What he needed was a gun.

"From now on," his wife said, "we set the alarm every night."

"Fine idea," he said. "If there's anything left."

"Maybe they're kids from the neighborhood," she said.

"Kids in the neighborhood are watching internet porn."

"You don't know anything about what kids are doing anywhere," she said. And there he'd done it again, accidentally pissed her off.

A faint brushing sound from below, like a cardboard box shoved across the hardwood floors. If they boxed the bottles from the wine cellar off the kitchen, the Ausone, Latour, Richebourg, and the Pingus, they were not kids.

"If we could call 9-1-1—" he said.

"Don't get on me about the phones."

"I appreciate that instead of slowly dying in bed from imaginary radiation I'll be shot at close range."

"You're a real asshole."

She'd said this before, called him a real asshole. What's the difference?

Alan needed a gun because he didn't know any martial arts, no karate, no jujitsu. He was not in good shape. He played tennis and golf, but not as sports. He was tan with a drinker's gut. In a white shirt and a pair of shorts and blue suede loafers and a vodka tonic and a cigar, he looked like a man in his midfifties who'd made enough in not entirely unscrupulous real estate for the younger wife and the Porsche and the house in Bel Air. He was in fact what he appeared to be. He could say that he had achieved beyond his wildest dreams, but he'd never had dreams as much as an instinct for buying and selling. And he knew when to wait out a situation. It troubled him that his human existence could be reduced to buying, selling, waiting. At times, lying in this bed in the dark, he hoped the exasperation he and his wife volleyed back and forth meant his wife hadn't tired of him as much as she felt caught in a similar roundabout. Oh, how he longed for a gun to protect her; wasn't that a sign of enduring love, of love endured? He couldn't quite be sure, certainty was her role.

His wife slid out of bed again in her silk nightgown. When they'd met, she slept naked. She paused, her head tilted as she listened to silence. Not now, but soon, he should tell her she looked beautiful without makeup.

"We can't let them get away with it," she said.

Alan lay there in bed with the covers up to his chin.

"If they were going to tie us up, or . . . whatever they do to people," he said—he didn't want to go that far, "they would've done it already so we wouldn't interrupt them."

"That's an odd way of thinking."

"It's logical," he said. "If we interrupt them, they'll have to deal with us, and we don't have a gun. Come back to bed."

"A gun!" she said.

He heard his car, his Porsche, backing up. His wife looked out the window.

"They're taking your car," she said.

"Let them have it. Come to bed."

"The bed won't protect us," she said. "This is *happening*, Alan, it's not a dream."

She wanted children and for years he'd said no. He told her when they married that he didn't want children, and she said afterward that older men always said that but then they changed their minds. For love. They reversed their vasectomies. For love. He didn't need a reverse vasectomy to prove he loved her. His tubes had never been cut off from the well. His wife was the only person he'd loved enough to marry. She felt right to him, was the only way he could explain it. They argued and he belittled her, and that was part of how they fit together. Give me a child, she said. You don't have to do anything. I'll do everything. But he had a father; he knew how it worked.

He felt safer in bed, as if the duvet could protect him with its force field of imported Turkish cotton. He was still a child. A child who wanted to protect his wife. If they made it through the night, she would always turn on the alarm and he would buy a gun.

It was a blessing they didn't have a baby. He could die and she could die, but harm a baby and he couldn't live with himself.

His wife peeked out the window.

"They're driving the Porsche out," she said, turning to follow the taillights down the driveway. "It's gone."

"We have insurance," he said. "It's over."

He didn't care about the Porsche, not one bit.

He got out of bed.

"I'll go down and call the police."

His wife stood at the window.

"Isn't that strange," she said. "They didn't look for my jewelry. If you hit a house like this, you'd expect diamonds."

"Hit a house?"

"It's fucking Bel Air."

The burglars had let her down.

The moonlight from the window lit half her face, the lines around her mouth, her thinning cheeks. She sighed as if the world sat on her slim shoulders. Why she had stayed with him and wasted her youth, he imagined was the central question of her therapy sessions. He hoped the therapist noted how well he supported her lifestyle, his willingness to go along with, if not respect, her notions about electromagnetic fields or, at the least, their trip to Majorca last summer. They spent a week at the beach; they lay side by side in the sun, looking out at the bright blue water, the men and women and even the kids bobbing in the sea. He'd reach out and hold her hand, and a few afternoons they fell asleep that way. His wife sunbathed topless in Majorca. Just like that, he remembered her golden skin. He felt the air flow back into his lungs.

"Who knows," he said. "They were car guys, somebody ordered a Porsche and they came up here and got one."

He put his arm around her, pulled her into his merlot gut, and she rested her head on his chest. He kissed her parted hair, smelled the flowery scent of her shampoo. Holding his wife was more comforting than lying under the imported Turkish cotton, her warmth against him felt like an indomitable force.

"I wish—" she started.

They both heard it, footsteps on the stairs.

Alan looked down at his wife and wished that he could not see her mouth agape, her eyes dark and panicked.

The footsteps took a left at the top of the stairs. They were fast and efficient; they were headed for the bedroom door.

Alan picked up Benjamin Franklin's biography from his nightstand, a thick hardcover book that he would never finish reading, a well-meaning and loathsome gift from his wife, and he waited beside the door. He lifted the book above his head because he intended to save himself and his wife with the breadth of Benjamin Franklin's life.

The footsteps paused at the door, as if readying themselves, then the doorknob turned. Alan recalled the movies: the knob turning and the hero's eyes wide and nervous but capable, and as the lock caught and the doorknob rattled against it, he wanted to be the hero. The rattling stopped, and Alan willed the footsteps to retreat, to sound off down the hallway and the stairs and out the back door and into the night. He counted silently, one, two, three, four, five, go, six, seven, go away, but then a shot (a shot!) blew out the door hardware and a figure dressed in black with a black ski mask, a head-sock with holes for the eyes and mouth, slipped into the bedroom and pressed a gun into his chest.

"Why don't you drop the Bible on the floor," the burglar said. The lips moved, the white skin around them just visible. The voice was surly. Alan smelled a chemical freshness, like the scented trees people hung from their car rearview mirrors.

Alan stood with his hands above his head, holding the book. The burglar poked his belly with the gun. They were the same height, looking eye to eye. But the burglar was skinny and amped. He rocked from one foot to the other as he pressed the gun into Alan.

"Put the book down," the burglar said.

"Alan," his wife called to him.

He'd forgotten about his wife! The gun felt hard and pointed against his gut. He let go of the book. *Thud*. The burglar waved the gun at him, directed him with it. Alan walked over to his wife. Like good hostages, they stood by the window barefoot and barely dressed. The burglar kept the gun on them as he looked around the bedroom, at their unmade bed, its cowhide headboard, the purple velvet-covered reading chairs, the ugly brass lamp picked out by his wife's designer. Then the boar's head over the faux fireplace. You can't buy class, is the line that came to mind when he looked at his bedroom through the burglar's eyes.

Alan put an arm around his wife. It was important the burglar see them as people because they were real people with real problems.

"We thought you'd left," Alan said.

The burglar peered through the doorway into the closet. His wife's jewelry, her four-carat diamond engagement ring, her diamond and sapphire earrings and necklaces and bracelets—the evidence that he supported his wife's lifestyle—were in the closet, locked in the safe. The jewelry guy had come for the diamonds after all.

"Take whatever you want," Alan said. "We'll stay right here."

"Shut up," the burglar said. He gestured again with the gun, directed them toward the closet, and they shuffled forward like an elderly couple. He turned on the light and they blinked at the brightness. One side was his and the other hers. Their clothes hung smartly on hangers. A black safe was bolted to the floor at the back of the closet. No one could move it out of the house; instead, they held you at gunpoint while you keyed in the code. Alan and his wife crept forward as if the closet were a passageway to an alternative night, where a masked man was not pointing a gun at their backs. As if they could sidle their way out.

"Stop there," the burglar said.

He swung the gun in front of his wife, and his free hand pointed at the safe.

"Open it," he said to her, and raised the gun to Alan's head. "And if you put in the panic code, he's dead."

The gun pushed into the soft flesh of Alan's temple.

Alan had paid extra to wire the safe for the panic code. If his wife punched a certain series of numbers on the keypad, the safe opened and alerted the police. He'd made his wife memorize the code, he'd tested her. Alan was naive. He was a consumer of safes instead of a protector of his home. The burglar knew about the panic code; he read about safes on the internet just like Alan.

His wife crouched by the safe. Her eyes looked like the hero's in the movies.

His wife was going to disobey the burglar.

"We don't have a panic code," Alan said.

"Bullshit," the burglar said, and then to his wife, "Open the safe."

His wife leaned close to the keypad and punched in numbers. The bolt clicked and she turned the lever handle and pulled open the door.

"Can we get you a bag?" Alan said.

The burglar handed his wife a blue floral-print pillowcase Alan recognized from the guest bedroom downstairs.

"Never mind," Alan said, and then the gun slapped him on the side of the head. He bowed forward, pain splintering his skull.

"Jesus!" his wife said.

"Shut up!" the burglar said.

"Please don't hurt him," his wife said. She was crying as she looted the safe. She scooped the diamonds and sapphires from the velvet trays and into the pillowcase. She sniffled.

Alan stayed bent over; he was closer to his wife this way, and if he stood he thought he'd throw up.

"I'm okay," he whispered to her.

"Oh, Alan," she said. They were so close, their heads almost touching, and he regretted the child. He wanted to give her a child. He touched her sweet-smelling hair and promised he would give his wife the child she wanted. He hoped it wasn't too late; he wouldn't let it be too late for them. The safe was empty, soon they would be free of the burglar and his gun.

Then he heard it, the siren in the distance.

The burglar looked at his wife.

"Bitch," he said.

"Please," Alan said, and fell to his knees. He would like to say he covered his wife's body with his, threw himself over her, protected her flesh with his own. But he knelt beside her and waited. He prayed the burglar would spare her the sight of Alan collapsed and bleeding while she waited for her bullet. He took her hand and whispered to his wife, "Majorca, Majorca," as if the word were code, but it was memory he was after, or a heaven's landscape, sun and sand and seawater, seagulls floating across blue skies. The gun pressed into the back of his head, and he tried to whisper again to his wife, to reassure her, but at that moment the back of his head exploded, and his body dropped forward against the safe, not that Alan could feel his face hit the reinforced steel door, he could feel only the seagulls, their soft feathers now fluttering inside him. He could not sense or imagine the blood pouring from his lopped-off head, or the spattering of skull fragments across the wall, or his wife screaming, a bloodcurdling scream if Alan could still feel his blood curdle but he could not. The burglar could and the burglar ran; he ran from the sound and the sight of death, he fled the scene. And in this way, Alan saved his wife.

ACKNOWLEDGMENTS

* * *

Thank you to the extraordinary writer Deesha Philyaw! I am so honored and profoundly grateful to you for choosing this collection for the Drue Heinz Literature Prize.

Thank you, Peter Kracht, Jane McCafferty, Alex Wolfe, Amy Sherman, Christine Ma, Joel W. Coggins, Lesley Rains, Kelly Lynn Thomas, John Fagan, and everyone at University of Pittsburgh Press for all the work on this book. Thank you, Drue Heinz, in memoriam, for your generosity, for encouraging us to write short stories and making a place for them.

Thank you to the editors who published some of these stories in their literary journals, kept the fire and hope alive, and the incredible Roxane Gay who picked the first, "Small in Real Life."

I am most grateful to the people I met at the Bennington Writing Seminars, especially my tremendous teachers Bret Anthony Johnston and Amy Hempel, Jill McCorkle, Askold Melnyczuk, and Lynne Sharon Schwartz, my friends there, and the community that started up the road from Shirley Jackson's house and continues onward.

To Yiyun Li for your kindness and getting me started. Thank you for your insights on writing as well as these stories, Garth Greenwell, Tom Barbash, Tom Drury, and Sheila Heti.

To Susan Pagani, so delighted to find you in Vermont, changed my writer life; and to Kate Milliken and Linda Michel-Cassidy for advice and unwavering support, and Dashka Slater for your clear notes.

To Amelia, Wyatt, and Oliver for, well, everything.

❋   ❋   ❋

Stories previously appearing in journals, sometimes in earlier forms: "God's Work," *The Southampton Review*; "Handbag Parade," *J Journal*; "Harmony," *Pembroke Magazine*; "Red Bluff," *Potomac Review*; "Small in Real Life," *PANK Magazine*; "The Spaniard," *Santa Monica Review*; and "Toucan," *Ascent*.